FORBIDDEN VICES

FORBIDDEN VICES

VICES

A CHARLIE REDMOND MYSTERY

MICHAEL L. DOUGLAS

MCP Books, Maitland, FL

MCP Books
2301 Lucien Way #415
Maitland, FL 32751
407·339·4217
www.MCPBooks.com

ISBN-13: 978-1-63505-292-3
LCCN: 2016915358

Distributed by Itasca Books

Printed in the United States of America

DEDICATION

To my late partner and husband in spirit, David Joseph McCaffrey, who possessed absolutely no forbidden vices . . . only cherished virtues.

ACKNOWLEDGEMENTS

A heartfelt and gratifying thanks to my professional partners in crime at the former Austin Medical Center in Austin, Minnesota (now, Mayo Health System - Austin), who have known about this novel since its conception in my creative mind. They are the highly capable and extremely well read nursing staff in the Urgent Care department who are muses in their own right. Much appreciation to Angelique Maricle, who took the time to introduce me to the entire team and show me the ropes. Thanks also to Debbie Bartness, Jenny Dryer, Gina Everson, Cheryl Gerhart, Jennifer Kraushaar, Lisa Robinson, and Jeanne Wright. Collectively, you have been a source of support and constant inspiration.

Many thanks to my husband, Paul, for putting up with my initial revisions and my incessant declarations of their greatness. Thank you for keeping me grounded.

Thanks to my spiritual brother-in-law, Richard A. McCaffrey, who always believed in me.

I am grateful to fellow Minnesota author Ellen Hart, whose instruction provided the spark that I needed to create.

I am most grateful to Michèle Davis and Jon Phillips. Not only were your critiques helpful, but both of you saw the possibilities for this series and introduced me to the world of publishing.

To all the rest of you who encouraged me and shared my enthusiasm and drive, thank you.

CHAPTER 1

Charlie Redmond could hear the coffeemaker beep three times from inside his riverfront bungalow. On cue, he freed himself from his outdoor exercise bar and jumped to the ground, eager to pour a cup that would, for the first time in over five years since moving north, not come with some sort of baggage. Soon, he'd have two months alone in New Zealand, without having to think about spending his downtime at lame singles' mixers. And there'd be no police reports, no need to call a fellow detective for yet another bitch session.

This morning, it was just the nectar of the gods and the *New York Times*. And a flight to New Zealand to look forward to. He'd been saving years for this vacation of a lifetime—two months in New Zealand fishing and extreme hiking. As soon as he finished his coffee and the paper, he'd pack, drop Thompson, his geriatric mutt, off at the neighbor's, and head to the airport. Charlie could savor it: his first transcontinental hiking sabbatical, even if he did dread twenty-four hours in coach.

As Charlie moved to the porch, he almost tripped over Thompson. The dog let out a pitiful yelp and went right back to sleep. Cup in hand, Charlie faced east, toward the Piscataqua River. He loved New Hampshire. He loved New England. He loved the outdoors. With so many things to love, who had time to stay indoors?

1

Ever since moving to Portsmouth from Boston he'd craved a change of pace. It was a brilliant day with a gentle breeze, so quiet that he could hear Thompson's slight snoring. Pulling the newspaper to him, Charlie glanced at the front page and took a satisfied sigh. Then he heard a noise. Whisper quiet, a black Escalade slowly pulled into his driveway, and a forty-something redhead emerged.

"Hello," she called. "Is there a Charles Redmond who lives here?"

Charlie quickly sized up the woman as she moved her sunglasses above her ponytail. Petite. Athletic. Inviting.

Something reminds me of Jenna . . .

"God, not now," he said almost imperceptibly.

"I'm sorry, what did you say?"

Another case, Charlie thought, as no one ever came to his home without invitation. No one. He lived among large swathes of NYC expats, many of them septuagenarians, who largely kept to themselves. He didn't mind adopting their isolationist tendencies. Although Charlie didn't mind the company of others from time to time, his ideal existence consisted only of himself and his trusty dog, Thompson. Life was much easier that way. No loose ends to deal with. No detective worth his salt likes loose ends.

Charlie's mind reeled. As much as he wanted to go on vacation, he couldn't actually refuse a case, could he? This was precisely the reason he moved north to New Hampshire from Boston. To flee the rat race and politics of law enforcement. Sure, he couldn't just cease what he'd been doing with conviction and pride for over fifteen years—the last few in Portsmouth. But his grand plan was a sound one. Work fewer and fewer cases for a couple of years, sock away money, and then terminate his Mickey Spillane shtick once and for all. No more cases. Nada. Never. End of story. He could focus full time on doing what he loved—competitive extreme hiking.

Yes—yes, of course, he *couldn't* take this case. He was just going to tell this person, this attractive, dainty female in a tailored gray pantsuit with manicured strawberry-red nails, that he was about to leave the country today, and nothing was going to stop him.

"Charlie, please." He held out his right hand, smiling. "How can I help you this fine morning?"

"I need you," she said. "I need you to help find my father's killer. It's been two years."

Charlie's mind swirled. A much-needed getaway was all he'd thought about this past year. Was he ready to postpone this opportunity—an opportunity he was fully mentally prepared to take—for someone he'd just met? And for a woman, no less?

Charlie's smile disappeared. It was a good thing he'd purchased refundable coach round-trip tickets.

CHAPTER 2

"Why don't you follow me inside?" Charlie asked. He felt the least he could do was make his guest comfortable. "Coffee?"

"No thanks." The woman smiled sweetly. "I'm Carla Willems."

Charlie turned her last name over his tongue, playing with the vowels, trying to capture facts that hovered at the edge of his brain. The name sounded familiar.

"This is a . . . cozy place," Carla said, downplaying the state of the living room, which doubled as a laundry hamper. "How long have you lived here?"

"Not too long. About five years," Charlie said

"Oh. Well, you have a nice place, anyway. A little small, but nice." Carla almost strained with obeisance.

"So how did you find out about me?" He decided to cut right to the chase.

"Steve Richards. You worked with him while you were still with the local police department. Steve's sister, Ingrid, gave me your information. We're both biochemists at Dartmouth."

"Steve. Yeah." Charlie nodded. Carla had beauty, and brains, to match. "He's been with the Portsmouth PD for twenty years, the past five years with me since I moved here. I'm retired from the force now. Steve's a great guy. I can't take your case, though."

"Oh?" Carla said. "He came across to me as certain you would accommodate me. If I paid the fee, of course. I can certainly pay you that amount . . . and probably more. I believe you'd be worth it."

At least she's making this a little easier to consider. Maybe she's worth the trouble.

"So why don't you want to hear about my case?" she asked.

"Because I'm finally going on vacation—two months. There's a reason there are clothes all over the furniture. I was just about to take out the old suitcase before you showed up." He was whining now, like a child.

Carla sighed. "All right, fine—I'll just wait until you get back."

Charlie stared at Carla. He needed this vacation. He'd been training like a dog on tough New Zealand–like terrain for over a year. On the other hand, Carla had been fucked around for twice that long. She needed closure. And he could always use the money. He needed a cool, fun case. Fun? Okay, meaty. A meaty case to justify canceling the trip to New Zealand. The extra money wouldn't hurt, either. He better not screw this up.

"Carla," he asked, "what exactly is it you want from me?"

"Like I said, my father was killed almost two years ago, not far from here," Carla said. "All I've gotten is the runaround. I can't be patient anymore."

"Let's sit," Charlie said. "Steve recommended me, huh?"

"Are you surprised? Steve told me that this was an unsolvable cold case, at least by the police. He told me you've solved a couple of cases the police just couldn't figure out."

A couple? Way more than that.

"Look," she said, her sadness apparent, "I really need to know what happened to my father. He . . . he was killed. Sitting at his desk. Doing what he loved." She looked down at the floor, arms crossed.

"Who was your father?" Charlie asked, careful not to reveal his interest just yet. Carla's damsel-in-distress temperament appealed to him, though he'd never admit it to her.

"Lyle Willems," she said.

"Yes. Yes. I recall the case. Lyle Willems, the medical device guy. He was murdered a year and a half ago. His company was behind that spinal device. The one that was guaranteed to cure back pain. Um, Medicine, Medical Technologies . . . wait, MedTec, is that right?" Charlie asked.

"Yes, that's right. His murder was all over the news for a few weeks, but just like that," Carla snapped her fingers, "no one cared. The police seemed to stop investigating. There were leads that went nowhere. He was just sitting at his desk, apparently. A coworker found him with a gash in his neck."

Charlie's mind raced. He wanted to put the trip on hold, but, shit, all that money he'd spent—what was it, five thou, six? He assumed he could recoup the cost of the plane fare. But, there were other expenses, too—money that he'd never get back. Deposits on fishing boats, tour guides, lodging . . .

The silence was tedious. "I'm sorry about all of this," Carla finally said, softly. "It's been two years. I guess I can wait a couple more months, for when you get back."

"I've always wondered about this case," Charlie said, slowly. "Always thought it was so cut and dry." He suddenly sat upright. "Forget it. I'm not going anywhere. If I took a vacation now, I couldn't relax. I'd be thinking about your father the entire time." While this wasn't completely true, as a chronically single guy, Charlie didn't want to disappoint Mr. Willems's attractive daughter.

"All right, I'm happy to get started, but first I need to check on some things, then I'll give you a call so we can talk. How does that sound to you?" Charlie asked.

Carla nodded. "I hope you understand why I'm asking you to investigate this case, Mr. Redmond … uh … Charlie. My dad, well, he was important. He dedicated his life to truly ending suffering from chronic disease. He used to brag about how much he could do for people without stepping foot inside of a medical school. He was a noble man." She paused. "I'm just . . . frustrated. No one is doing *anything*. No one seems to care about this case anymore."

Charlie rose to pour another cup of coffee and was careful to measure his words. "Carla, although your father's case *is* cold, it *is* still solvable. I know it's been two years without a lead, but the Portsmouth Police Department has limited resources. I'm excited to have a look at this case, see what I can see."

Carla looked down at the ground, and walked toward the living room door. "Well, I'm glad such a seasoned private investigator is going to tackle my dad's death."

"Retired detective . . . and you never know what'll happen with a fresh pair of eyes," Charlie said, handing her an old business card. "Sometimes a new morsel of information is all that's needed to kindle a spark that'll lead somewhere."

"Call me the moment you get that spark," she said. She smiled weakly and made her way outside to her car.

CHAPTER 3

"I'm sorry," said the travel agent, "but we're unable to refund the cost of the airline tickets. We can, however, offer you airline miles."

Shit. Charlie steeled himself, then sighed. He had better things to do than to worry about eating the cost of the airfare—like calling his police buddy, Steve Richards.

"Steve. It's Charlie."

"Ah, the Great One!" Richards said when he picked up. "Oh, master of investigators near and far. Well, that didn't take long. What did you think of Carla?"

"First of all, Steve, I'm a retired detective formerly of the Portsmouth PD, not Philip Marlowe or Sherlock Holmes, okay?" Charlie began. "And, number two, she stole my vacation."

"What vacation?"

"I was off to New Zealand for a couple of months. I thought you knew!"

"What? I'm supposed to be your keeper now?"

"Why do you do this to me, Steve? You should be kissing my ass, assuming I'd take this case, you sonofabitch."

Richards gave a hearty laugh. "Hey, you're forgetting something. You need the info I have to crack this two-year-old cold case. If we couldn't solve it, what the

11

hell makes you think you can without a little help from the department? And what's in this for me?"

Charlie rolled his eyes. "All right. You could start by sending me the police report on the Lyle Willems murder, the autopsy results, pretty much whatever else you've got."

"Again, what's in this for me?"

"A big wet kiss after it's solved," Charlie laughed.

***

After he got off the phone Charlie quickly showered, searched the piles of clothes on the floor for something resembling a clean T-shirt and cargo pants, and propped himself in front of his computer. As he Googled Lyle Willems, pages and pages of hits displayed, and practically every article lauded his ascension through life. Charlie's memory was foggy, but he remembered the hubbub about Willems in the newspaper.

Charlie read through the basics: Willems grew up an only child in Brooklyn, poor and raised by a single parent. His career started with lemonade stands and matriculated to medical sales—durable goods, not pharmaceuticals. He apparently was skilled at establishing contracts with local vendors in the New York tristate area, and eventually operations expanded and he took on partners. Over time some people left as Willems demanded efficiency and loyalty every step of the way. Nothing punitive, it sounded like, just Willems asserting his personal value set of hard work and persistence.

Once his company, MedTec, grew enough to blanket the entire mid-Atlantic region and New England, Lyle

Willems enlisted various business and accounting partners. He eventually shed these partners when MedTec grew to a nationwide presence. Lyle opted to keep MedTec's flagship offices in New Hampshire, the largest of which was in Portsmouth. Charlie didn't live far from the scene of the crime.

MedTec was responsible for bringing some of the most innovative medical devices to market, revolutionizing numerous medical and surgical procedures, including cardiothoracic surgery, neurosurgical therapies, and most recently, spinal interventions. At the time of his death, Lyle Willems was in the midst of marketing a spinal device that could effectively eradicate chronic low back pain in patients, alleviating the need for unnecessary surgeries.

Obituaries from coast to coast lauded Willems's visionary abilities, and lamented his untimely death as a cruel and unexpected detour from the visionary prowess many in the industry bestowed upon him. Company employees lionized him, politicians and policymakers championed him, and physician lobby groups worshipped him. All of which made his murder completely improbable. Who would want him dead?

Before channeling his efforts elsewhere, Charlie found a spate of personal information. Willems's first wife died in a plane crash shortly after their wedding. His second wife, Emily, and their only child, Carla, were his only surviving family. Emily Willems had been married before, and she had a son, Guy, she brought into her marriage to Willems.

By now, Charlie had completely forgotten about boarding a plane to New Zealand. He shook his proverbial fist. "If the goddamn police can't close this case, then it's up to me. If only for Carla's sake." Carla had no other options. Charlie Redmond had many options. Now was the time to put them to use.

CHAPTER 4

Before he could really start investigating, Charlie had to stop over at old lady Bainbridge's, his neighbor/dog sitter, to cancel her services. Bainbridge was an eccentric sixty-something spinster who lived a couple of bungalows down the street. She actually had a first name, but he could never remember what it was. It didn't matter. She didn't care. Whenever he greeted her on a short jog, her taciturn voice asking him what was good about the day made Charlie think he wasn't going to say Good morning to Ms. Bainbridge ever again.

He rapped hard on the sexagenarian's front door. Not cop-knock hard, but hard enough to rattle the old gal. "Hello, Ms. Bainbridge," Charlie said, "Just stopped by to let you know I won't be giving you my dog for two months after all. Something came up, as it always does with me."

After he explained the situation, she puckered her lips. "Eh. Was countin' on that money for a couple of things. What the hell'm I 'spose to do now?" Charlie didn't know how to respond, especially with her six-foot-two-inch frame glaring down at him as though she were staring down the barrel of a gun.

"Um, look, I can loan you some money," Charlie said.

"Whatever. I won't forget this total breach of trust. Was beginning to warm to you as a neighbor."

"But we hardly ever speak," Charlie replied, and Bainbridge looked at him as though this were a revelation. Her beady eyes glared at him with a shine, as if she'd been crying, but her eyelids didn't move; matter of fact, he didn't think she ever blinked.

"Yeah, have it your way. I'll remember this moment if you have another favor to ask of me. I will. Don't doubt me," she said, unblinking.

"I'll keep a mental note," Charlie half-jokingly replied, thinking that Bainbridge was a story that could write itself. He knew he'd have to call her eventually to dog sit, but for now his mind was on the Willems case and who would want to do the old patriarch harm.

Charlie got into his big brown boat, a 1985 Lincoln Town Car. It may not have been flashy, but it was reliable, and if anyone hit him, well, they'd have a scrunched-up tin can for a car after hitting his built-solid-in-Detroit jalopy. Heading to downtown Portsmouth, which was only a short drive from his place near the river, Charlie drove north. He thought about Carla's address on her business card, 723 Springbrook Lane. The highway led him past well-worn New England tourist favorites nestled in pristine countryside. Portsmouth was a working-class city with an opulent feel. For every Ford Focus, there was a Lexus sedan or high-end SUV, much like Carla's, sharing the road. A healthy mixture of the proud, libertarian worker and erudite university type sophisticate described the average southern New Hampshirite.

Charlie thought back to Shelby, a former female client. Shelby claimed her husband had been two-timing her with a "tart" almost half her age. When Charlie had trailed Shelby to her trailer park home, he'd seen Shelby, her husband, and another woman, who seemed strung out, get into an altercation. When the unidentified woman swung a baseball bat over her head, Tarzan-like, Charlie had raced to the trailer and lunged himself at Shelby's husband—but not before getting hit by a bullet in the right arm by Shelby. At that moment, everything made sense. The entire fucking trailer was a pot farm, and Shelby intended to lure Charlie there, shoot him and the other woman, and claim they both tried to steal her weed. She'd then leave the country with her white-trash husband and sell the stash. Charlie learned a valuable life lesson that night: never completely trust a damsel in distress, especially if she was an attractive one.

Something wasn't entirely squaring with Carla, in Charlie's mind, like the situation with Shelby. Trust between client and detective was paramount, and Charlie wasn't going to make the same mistake now. He needed to know a little more about her, needed to resolve lingering uncertainty about her motivations. He didn't like what he was about to do, and he hoped she wasn't at home. For the moment, this was Charlie's agenda. At least Carla had the decency to tell him that she had one too. And, unlike Shelby, she actually had a brain.

Charlie sighed and pulled up across from 723 Springbrook Lane. Dusk made it tougher to note the architectural particulars, but he saw that it was a nicely kept one-story rambler. He continued, knowing he needed to find out more about Carla and any other clues as to her motivations for finding her father's killer— even if she wasn't at home. A quick survey around the fenced perimeter suggested no one was home. He noticed, after opening and making his way through the unlocked chain-link fence and peering through a few of the windows, that all the lights were off.

Relief.

As far as Charlie could tell, the house had two bedrooms and one bath, owned by a single (perhaps divorced) female. Maybe a dependent in tow, but not likely. A well-kept garden in the immediate front yard and small vegetable garden in back meant a diligent, industrious person who saw things through. But the unlocked front gate meant she was a little careless, even naïve. That didn't quite fit. In fact, this made Charlie a little nervous. In all his years as a detective he couldn't recall just sauntering onto a subject's property with such ease. He took advantage of the opportunity and made his way toward the back patio door, which was unencumbered by curtains or blinds.

He stretched out his right hand for the sliding door handle with mixed feelings. Although the only other entrance to the house, the front door, was secure, could it be possible that he could forgo picking the lock if, by chance, the patio door were unlocked? His palms were sweaty as he grasped the sliding door handle. It gave way, and he entered the rear of the house via the kitchen. Nobody was home. Lights off. Why would a seemingly regimented person leave the house unsecured like this? Charlie made his way toward the living room area, wondering if he would have to break out his phone to provide some light to guide him. He froze. He felt a strange bushy sensation on his bare right leg. Looking down, he saw a chubby calico cat sizing him up. He let out a major sigh of relief.

Charlie broke out his phone to use as a flashlight. He moved on, with the calico right behind him purring with curiosity. On the couch lay various typed papers, some crumpled or folded, and others terrorized by a red pen. These looked to be part of something, perhaps a manuscript, she was editing. He picked up a random page.

I feel like the emotions in me are increasingly unpredictable. I honestly don't know how I'm able to function at work. Sometimes you just can't understand why your marriage failed. . . . You try to move on. You try to be happy. But the emptiness comes in waves, sometimes daily. Yes, at times divorce brings introspection . . . and other times, complete social deprivation. God, I sound so desperate.

And Dad . . . God, I wish my father were still alive. When he died, so much of my reason for living, for happiness, for a purpose on this earth, died too. I know that if he were still on this earth, he'd support me completely. I know that he's watching over me. I feel his spirit every day. My father would want me to take charge of my life, even if that means doing whatever I had to do find out why he had to die. . . ."

Charlie knew exactly what was happening to Carla in terms of the divorce. He'd been through it himself. He read further.

A loss. That's what this legal separation, this break, this escape from vows that were supposed to be lifelong really means. A total loss. Sometimes, it's all I can do to wrap myself up in research and work. I need to reconnect with society, with my life. Give it meaning. I really need to find something, anything fundamentally good for me.

Charlie heard a noise just a few feet away at the front door. *Carla!* He threw down the paper and flew toward the sliding glass door. Once outside, he fled through the alley, narrowly escaping an oncoming light truck. Sweat rolled down his face as he realized he didn't have time to latch the sliding patio door. He hoped she wouldn't notice later—her being careless and all. He walked around the back of the houses on Springbrook Lane and slid into his Lincoln, trying to look at home in case anyone saw him loitering in the alley.

Back on the highway, with his window down, he thought more about Carla's words. Carla needed more than just a damn good retired detective to attack the case: she needed to do good by herself. He couldn't imagine her series of misfortunes: marriage, then divorce, the stress of the unsolved murder of her father. She was making an effort at resolving all these feelings. Finding her father's killer was a step in that direction. Charlie could kick himself for suspecting her of screwing him in some way, but he had to be sure about her intentions for hiring him. He had the memory of Shelby to thank for his suspicions. No, this didn't seem to be the same thing that happened with him and Shelby. Carla was good; she wasn't withholding anything. His mind could rest and do the job, for her … and for Jenna.

CHAPTER 5

The following morning, a package arrived for Charlie from the Portsmouth PD. He walked out onto the porch and leafed through the contents: autopsy findings, persons interviewed about the murder, and various police reports. Richards had given him some good, solid information to consider, which made his job a little easier.

Charlie began with the police reports. Lyle Willems was found dead at his desk in MedTec's Portsmouth headquarters around 7:00 a.m. on a Saturday morning. The estimated time of death was midnight Friday. He was found by a MedTec engineer, Brian Gardner. According to Gardner, Willems's body was situated as if he were resting, his back causing the desk chair to recline at an extreme angle backward. His head was hyperextended over the back of the chair. There was no headrest, and Willems's body looked unnatural, which suggested that whatever happened to Willems didn't occur at the beginning of a non-traditional workday. The deep gash on the left side of Willems's neck resulted in a prolonged bleed, but wasn't profound enough to hit deeper structures, like bone. The autopsy findings said the wound was probably the result of significant force, meaning that the neck wound may not have killed him.

In other words, he could have died by some other means before he was stabbed.

Multiple other interviews corroborated that Willems had left the office on the Friday night he was murdered. No one ever saw him return to his office. Although some coworkers came in to work on the weekends, Willems had no time for type A's staying late on a Friday, much less coming in on Saturday morning to get things done. He always advocated for diligence during the week, but felt just as strongly that the weekend was for a life outside the office. If Willems violated his own work ethic by coming in on Friday night, or never leaving in the first place, it's possible that no one ever saw him.

There was truth to this argument. Charlie noted from other statements that the security guards had been reprimanded many times before for numerous problems: possession of alcohol on duty, sleeping at assigned posts, and even leaving whole office suites unsecured. The entire crew working that night had been fired over Willems's murder.

Brian Gardner wasn't the only employee who came in on weekends, but Friday night usually meant the facility was a tomb. Did the killer know about logistical office missteps on a typical Friday night, or was he or she just lucky? All employees had access to the home office 24/7, either via a key or some sort of electronic code that allowed entry. Willems believed in work-life balance, but wasn't going to stand in the way of an odd off-hours creative spark.

Charlie had seen scenarios like this unfold in cut-throat industries where company secrets were guarded like gold. Political operations, tech organizations, and other high-profile industries by their nature could foster murder within their ranks. But medical device companies? Maybe. Why would they be any different?

Looking through the documents, Charlie understood why the case quickly went cold. There wasn't any credible evidence—no prints at the crime scene, no proof of any employees who didn't have to be there that day. Willems's past was about as clean as it could be. Charlie couldn't find any bad business relations or deals, nor hints of an extramarital affair. His erratic work hours were just part of his personality and work ethic. He was dedicated to his passion: inventing and patenting medical devices that would someday help patients. No one had any reason to suspect Willems was guilty of anything other than being a fiercely dedicated executive.

However, the report did name a person of interest, a man who owned a small advertising agency in Portsmouth, located close to MedTec HQ. Lawrence Ash and his company, Ashton Advertising, mainly worked with a range of clients that included medical device and pharmaceutical companies. Ashton Advertising competed with other ad agencies for the types of potentially lucrative accounts that would feature blockbuster products. Ash was questioned repeatedly by detectives in the days following the murder, as there were numerous tips from MedTec employees that Ash's business sense was a direct result of his "obsession" with MedTec products and innovation. One employee interviewed said Ash's behavior was "just plain creepy." Ash would ingratiate himself to Willems at every opportunity, showing up at MedTec company meetings unannounced, and constantly badgering the HR department for a corporate appointment, even though his business had no active or pending accounts involving therapeutic medical devices. Willems obviously hadn't appreciated a puppy latching on to his purse strings and getting rich off his efforts.

Police had stopped considering Ash a person of interest three months later. Ultimately, it had been a fruitless lead. Motive was key, so what would be the motive? Love? Hate? Jealousy?

Charlie retrieved Carla's professional card. He thought one last time about the New Zealand trip, shook his head, and smiled. He grabbed his phone. He made the right decision. It was time for him to help Carla with hers. The reports that Steve Richards sent to Charlie were helpful and gave him stable theories to work with. He couldn't wait to put some of his musings into motion, especially since it involved meeting with Carla again. He called her to arrange a get-together.

CHAPTER 6

Carla was more than an hour late to their lunch meeting at Henrietta's Bistro, and Charlie could feel his irritation rise.

Keep it cool, act nonchalant.

He watched a cruise ship sail into Portsmouth Harbor. He checked his watch. Just as he was about to call all his theories about her into question and bolt, Carla strolled in, as gorgeous as he remembered.

"Hi," she said, barely disguising the anxiety in her eyes. Her strawberry-blond ponytail swung as she sat down. "I'm so sorry I'm late. I should've called you. I'm just so nervous about reopening my father's case, it's hard for me to sit here across from you, let alone meet you here. I almost wanted to cancel the whole thing. But, I'm glad I came. I really want it to be solved."

Charlie was reassured. "It's no problem at all," he said, once they sat. "I've been doing my research on your father. He wasn't only well liked, but he was very dedicated to his organization."

"My dad's entire life revolved around doing as much as he could for patients and making their lives much easier. He was so oriented to others, he never had time for himself. When I was growing up, during summer breaks from school," Carla continued, "Dad would take me to one of his offices and let me just hang out

25

while he worked. I loved playing secretary and using the typewriter, pens, carbon paper . . . sometimes the Dictaphone. I don't think he cared what I did, just as long as I had fun creating."

"How long did he do this? Did you stop coming eventually?" Charlie asked her, genuinely curious about her life.

"Well, as I got older, I found I had other interests . . . things that were much more important and gratifying than going to some office. Studying, boys, drinking—you know, all the normal stuff an ambitious, overachieving high school girl needed to justify her existence."

Charlie smiled. "Yeah, 'cept in my case, you could replace studying with booze, boys with girls, and drinking with more booze. You'd have my raison d'être right there."

Carla laughed, and Charlie continued, "But back to your story. What about college, or afterward? Did you just lose interest in your father's career?"

"No, I always kept in touch, and as time went on, I knew he was always on solid footing, that he was gratified with his career. From the time I applied to grad school, I guess, I didn't stay in contact with him as much as I should have, especially since I got married." She paused then added, "Well. I'm not married now. I mean, I used to be. I went through a divorce recently." Carla paused for longer. "I'm sorry. I should have told you. Crazy."

"No problem. I understand," Charlie replied. "I've been there myself. It's okay."

Carla blushed. "I don't mean to burden you with these details. I just want to express myself. It's therapeutic. In fact, I'm writing a book about it now."

I know. I read some of it.

Charlie chuckled, feeling uncomfortable. She continued, "By the time he was murdered, I hadn't kept up my end of the bargain. It was probably a good four or five years since I had spent any quality time with Dad." Tears sprang up at the corners of her eyes, and Charlie could tell she was fighting them back.

"And your mother?" Charlie asked. "Do you still have a relationship with her?"

"I never felt especially close to Mom. You know, she was Dad's second wife. He remarried after his first wife was killed in a plane crash." Charlie nodded. "Don't get me wrong, I love my mother. But I always felt a certain kinship, more of a special bond, with my father. Well, intellectually, anyway." She again fought back tears, and Charlie resisted the urge to comfort her. "I miss him so much."

Charlie was growing more saddened for Carla with each word. Not usually prone to emotion, he was stifling tears himself.

"I may not have been as close to my father when he was killed," Carla said. "But my mom was there for him, and she supported him through all his endeavors. She's been hit hard by this."

"Tell me, Carla. I know about your father's creative role in his enterprise. But did he have any other duties, or give himself any other roles?" Charlie asked.

"My father ran MedTec like any other CEO with an eye on the bottom line. But he also stressed creativity when it came to establishing contacts and signing contracts. With him, it was all about the presentation of the product to clients. He often said the way a MedTec product looked 'reeled 'em in and hooked 'em.'"

"Okay, if they were about to release a product, wouldn't your father have to sign off on it?"

"Well, sure. It didn't matter how small. If it were a cure for any illness, my father was completely involved in the product's development. Anything that didn't pass muster either went right back to the drawing board, or was in danger of being scrapped altogether."

"All right, so if your father didn't have his hands dirty with a potential product, it wasn't going to get produced," Charlie said.

"Not exactly, at least not at first. MedTec had to grow as a company. My dad as CEO needed the input of many minds and personalities. But over time, contacts began to favor only Dad's ideas on marketing and production. He eventually didn't need partners or advisers for guidance. He really had the Midas touch." Carla squinted, looking keen and alert, clearly enjoying telling this part of the tale. Then her eyes darkened. "Initially, the police and detectives did suspect a connection with Dad's workplace."

"There was someone named Lawrence Ash, who crashed a lot of company meetings," Charlie said, not letting on how he knew about Ashton Advertising. Lucky for him, Carla didn't inquire.

"Right," Carla said. "Larry was the only lead that detectives had at the outset."

The waitress brought their food, and Carla's gaze traveled toward the floor, toward Charlie's legs. "You look like a well-traveled gentleman," she said, clearly needing to change the topic.

Charlie blushed. "Thank you. Is it *that* obvious?" He didn't wait for Carla to reply. "I'm an outdoors type. I love to hike. Extreme hiking, mostly. That's what I was planning to do before you suddenly popped into my life. Was all set on going to New Zealand that day, actually."

"Wow . . ." Carla said. "I honestly don't know what to say."

"Don't say anything," Charlie said. "Just know that your father's there, watching down on you . . . us."

Aware of Charlie's slight disappointment, Carla stressed her gratitude on Charlie's decision to take her father's murder case, and said, "A detective that also likes to be one with nature. Interesting. You certainly don't fit the mold."

Charlie didn't know whether to be offended or complimented. He decided not to say anything as he took his first bite of his BLT.

***

After lunch, Charlie walked Carla to her SUV. "I know what I can do," she said. "I'll get in touch with the facility manager at MedTec, Ken Dougherty. He's super. He should be able to lead you in the right direction."

Charlie liked her initiative. "Sounds great."

"Ken was one of the company's first hires. He's been there for over twenty-five years. He's got the battle scars to prove it."

"I'm intrigued. Battle scars?"

"Ken's been through all of the company's trials and triumphs and has somehow risen above it all. Was loyal to Dad all the way. You'll really like him."

Charlie smiled at the thought.

"I know you said you'll start with MedTec, but maybe you can multitask?" asked Carla.

Damn, she read my mind.

"Yep, I plan on finding out more about Lawrence Ash. Also your mom, Emily."

"Whoa," Carla said. "You've already got a to-do list, apparently."

"I'm sorry, do you have concerns about my wanting to find out more from your mother?"

"No, no. A detective's got to follow the leads that beckon. You're the boss in this situation. I just want to help find my father's killer."

Carla got into her Escalade and sat for a while before starting the vehicle, talking to Charlie through the open driver's side window. "I really do hope Ken can help you. I can't think of any better source for you right now."

"Well, if he's as willing as you say he is, it'll be of benefit to both of us," Charlie said.

Carla looked at Charlie and nodded. Charlie returned her gaze with intensity. The more time he spent with Carla, the more resolved he became to track down Lyle Willems's killer.

CHAPTER 7

A couple of days later, after going for an early morning run, Charlie headed toward MedTec headquarters in downtown Portsmouth. He drove south and east on Market Street, hung a right at Congress Street, and finally took another right farther south at Tanner Street. Before him was a ten-story art deco building, complete with large front-facing windows, a taupe exterior, and huge symmetrical trapezoidal shapes adorning each story on all sides. Directly above the entrance, about three stories up, blazed the blood-red signage: MEDTEC.

He managed to parallel park in between a couple of company minivans across the street, both of which bore the company logo and the tagline "Innovation Without Frustration." Charlie got out of his Lincoln and made his way toward the front of the company building, which featured a modified enclosed area—a patio of sorts. The double door leading out to the patio swung open, and Carla emerged.

"You found it! I'm so glad to see you, Charlie."

Charlie shook her hand, fighting the urge to hug her.

"This building is unique," she said, "a testament to Dad's vision and creativity. Let's go in."

As they stood in the lobby, Charlie looked around, making mental notes. The reception area reminded him of a bustling hotel lobby—employees coming and going, amid various museum-quality sculptures and floor figurines. The walls were covered with posters, paintings, and motivational propaganda. "Your father certainly had many ways of expressing himself," he said.

"Pretty wild, huh? A little difficult to avoid it. He wanted to make sure that everyone who worked within these walls channeled their loyalty to the company's goals through hard work and dedication to Dad's vision of stamping out disease with medical devices."

Carla showed Charlie the second floor, which housed the company's various divisions. The cardiovascular section, abdominal surgical section, and orthopedic surgical section made up the three largest occupied spaces on the floor, each complete with its own conference room and associated office.

Carla led Charlie to the center portion of the second floor—a glass-enclosed hexagonal structure with a desk occupying one side. Across from the desk sat a series of shelves, adorned with reference books and industry trophies. "This is . . .was Dad's office. It's remained empty since his death. No one really wants to take the initiative and convert it. I suppose it's kept as some sort of tribute. I really don't mind, especially when you take a look around and see the results of his labors." Carla pointed to the trophy-filled shelves, referring to the many accolades Willems received during his professional life with the company. Her voice trailed off, and Charlie could tell she was suppressing tears.

They ascended to the third floor, which was mostly empty, its various rooms either abandoned or filled with boxes of unused office furniture. The exception was a small room to the north side of the floor, adjacent to the elevators, where a short, portly man sat hiding behind his computer. He rose when they approached, his tight plaid shirt straining against its top five buttons. Charlie noticed his jeans were a little more forgiving. The man stuck out his right hand. "Hello! I'm Ken Dougherty!"

Carla had informed Charlie that Dougherty was a never-married male without children, totally devoted to Lyle and his mission for the company, almost a syco-phantic personality. He didn't have much of a life out-side work, which gave him time to gossip about others. He seemed always "in the know" within the company.

Charlie returned the handshake. "Charlie Redmond."

"You must be having a great day today, Ken," Carla joked, "or are you always this excited to meet private detectives?" Dougherty shot her a blank look.

"I'm actually a retired detective of the Portsmouth PD," Charlie said.

"Okay, well," Carla began, embarrassed, "I'll leave you two to talk about important things." She whispered at Charlie. "Are you sure you can handle Ken?"

I'm a damn police detective. I've been in much more precarious situations. Charlie smiled back at her and nodded.

"So, Mr. Redmond, what can I do for you?" Dougherty asked. "Who do you want to speak with first?"

Dougherty was essential, at least that's how Carla regarded him, Charlie thought. Although other employees may have thought he was always ingrati-ating toward Lyle Willems, he was thought of by Lyle as a confidant and always had Lyle's ear about com-pany product trends. He was a person whose position within the company was the conduit for much-needed information.

"It's Charlie, please. How about I start with you, Ken?"

"Oh, I'd love to oblige. But why don't we talk last? I was in the middle of something when you popped in with Carla."

"Okay," said Charlie, "let's start with the person who found Mr. Willems murdered. Brian Gardner."

Charlie had barely finished with his request when Dougherty got on the phone. "Brian, it's Ken Dougherty. The gentleman I was telling you about earlier is here. Please be as cooperative as possible and answer his questions." With that, he hung up, winked at Charlie, and said, "Brian is ready when you are."

Charlie was amazed at this guy's energy. Was he always this hyped up? How much influence did he have in the company? He seemed beneficial to Charlie at this stage of the investigation. He wanted to speak to Dougherty first, but he'd find a way to make it through the other interviews quickly. Dougherty winked at Charlie. "I'll see you later, sir!"

CHAPTER 8

Brian Gardner sat across from Charlie in one of the empty rooms adjacent to Ken Dougherty's office, rubbing his hands on his jeans, a staple of the casual dress code Lyle Willems enforced in the company to inspire creativity among the employees. Charlie couldn't tell if his discomfort was from the metal folding chair and lack of windows, or his unease with the whole inquisition thing.

"I'm glad I could speak with you here," Charlie began.

"Sure. Likewise." Gardner looked up at the ceiling. Then down at his shoes.

Is he waiting for me to ask him another question before he even looks up at me? "I'm up here, Brian," Charlie said.

"Uh, sorry."

Charlie moved on. "So you stumbled upon Mr. Willems that Friday night?"

"It was Saturday morning," Gardner said, not hiding his irritation at the question.

Damn, this kid's paying attention.

Gardner continued, a little less nervous. "Yes, I found Mr. Willems. He was sitting at his desk. I was the only one—well, I thought I was the only one—in the office then. Other than Mr. Willems, obviously."

"But he was dead, so that really doesn't count," Charlie said.

"Yep," Gardner said. He looked up at the ceiling again, before settling upon Charlie's gaze. He was describing the scene, stuff Charlie already knew. Yet he continued his interrogation, becoming more cynical and less optimistic about his interviewee.

"Okay, so you saw Lyle Willems resting in his chair in an unusual position. You had to go in and investigate?"

"Yep," Gardner said, "and I spoke his name a couple of times. But, don't get me wrong. I didn't touch him, or anything, because the whole scene was looking pretty weird."

"So then you called the cops?"

"Yep. Because it was the right thing to do, of course."

Jesus, save the piety for the pulpit.

"Did you know Lyle Willems, you know, on a personal level?"

"Well, no. Not really," he said, showing a hint of frustration. "We only talked a couple of times to discuss a product that was eventually abandoned."

"Did you talk about anything else after the project was abandoned, as you say?"

"Well. Um, my finding another line of work, um, possibly."

Charlie had to suppress a laugh. Gardner grew crimson.

"Thanks for speaking with me, Brian," Charlie said. "You've been a great help."

"Really? I have?"

Charlie smiled.

***

Charlie next sat down with an engineer named Ted Barker—one of the creative types within MedTec Willems tried so hard to nurture. Ted's unkempt beard and ponytail, which landed mid-back, were predominantly gray with specks of natural black hair throughout. His thin black eyebrows contrasted sharply with his alabaster New Hampshire skin. His coarse golden bracelets—"peace bands," as he called them—added to the geeky, hippie vibe.

"I'm glad you're able to speak with me today."

"Sure thing, Detective. Wow," said Ted, "this is so prime. A real-life detective, like in *Law and Order*. You've gotta be busy 24/7 what with all the cases you're probably workin'."

"Actually, I'm not an active detective. I'm retired. So, I've got the time to get to the bottom of things." He noticed a square-shaped steel mechanism in Barker's right palm. "A stress reliever of some sort?"

"Oh, this thing? It's actually part of a much larger medical device that never left the planning stage a couple of years ago. The hope was to create a special interlocking instrument that could deliver thermal therapeutic massage to areas of the body affected by chronic pain. It's just another one of my brilliant ideas down the crapper. Some potential clients don't want to take chances, I suppose." Barker laughed.

Charlie switched gears from Barker's self-deprecation to the matter at hand and asked, "Did you work with Lyle Willems?"

"Sure did. I wish I would have worked with him more on this project," he said, referring to the steel block in his hand, "but a different production team never got the idea in front of him. Then he was killed. That was unfortunate."

"Why?" Charlie asked.

"You know, a company has its leaders. But some leaders are so much more gifted, going over and beyond the call of duty. That was Mr. Willems. Everyone who had the chance to work with him, from initial product development up to launch, cherished the experience."

"So, he was fair and highly capable?"

"Without a doubt. He was totally committed to seeing something he believed in all the way through, from beginning to end. And he made sure that each person in the production team counted. He made us realize there were no weak links. He was awesome. Say, check this. Have you ever heard of the BioDerm Aortic Valve?"

Charlie was sorry to say that he hadn't. But science and engineering weren't exactly his strong suits. Barker wasn't dissuaded. "Aw man, it was only one of the most important cardiac valve replacement devices to hit the market within the past five years. It revolutionized the cardiothoracic surgical treatment for all diseases that affected the aortic valve. Patient survival rates increased practically overnight." Barker's eyes grew wide.

"Anyway," he continued, "those who were involved in this particular product launch, including a very lucky colleague of mine, knew that Mr. Willems saw the potential for this device. Somehow, I don't know how, but somehow, Mr. Willems got word that another production company was bringing a similar device to market. There was a timeline. We had to get all of our ducks in a row and present early specs to potential manufacturers. Mr. Willems basically trusted us with our innovations. Sure, we held many meetings that were secure and closely guarded, but in the medical device biz, any info could leak at any time. Didn't matter, Mr. Willems was on it. Somehow he was able to find out about the competitor's development timeline, undermine it, rally the troops here at MedTec, and bring the device to market, where it's consistently been one of our biggest sellers. He instilled confidence in the employees here. He is so missed."

Charlie looked at Barker. He was captivated by Barker's story, told with enthusiasm and passion.

"Then came the numerous awards and accolades for the product," Barker said. "As a company, we were already on the map, so to speak. But, boy, this device really put MedTec over the top. More and more lucrative contracts, national expansion of regional branch offices, my God, it was corporate nirvana! Always Mr. Humility, Mr. Willems didn't want all the credit for landing the aortic valve contract. He even returned the plaques and trophies and insisted that the names of all the team members be included on those awards. Just so freaking selfless, that man."

Charlie thought about Ted Barker's account of Willems.

Whoa, he really knocked himself over communicating his feelings in support of Lyle Willems. Drama included. Seems as though Lyle cast quite a blanket of influence over his employees, team members, and developers, even at the expense of possible ethical lapses. Possibly infiltrating the enemy camp to scoop a blockbuster product development? At the very least, it took massive balls on his part.

"Gotta say, Lyle showed a tremendous display of commitment. It's impressive," Charlie said. "It was a little risky, though. I suppose you really don't know how something like that will play out in the court of public opinion, at least with the company."

"Sure," Barker said, "but it was all good. Mr. Willems had our total loyalty. Risk be damned. Determination and commitment to success by way of teamwork, passion, loyalty, and enthusiasm were the qualities that defined him. He lived for that."

Charlie appreciated Barker's words, but the story gave him little new information. He thanked Ted for his interview and spoke with several other employees. The interviews were solid, but they didn't give Charlie any more mojo. What he needed was red meat, something concrete to move this thing forward. He didn't have to wait long. Up next was Alfred Jenkins.

CHAPTER 9

Alfred Jenkins, the sixty-something owner of AJ Diagnostics, was someone Carla had urged Charlie to talk to. Since Alfred wasn't part of the Lyle Willems family, Charlie had to seek him out at his office in Portsmouth's east side. According to the company's website, the "AJ" stood for Alfred Jenkins. His company wasn't part of MedTec, but existed within the same market—medical devices. While both companies weren't in direct competition with each other, both owners knew of each other. Lyle's was the more successful of the two.

When Charlie got to Jenkins's office, he encountered old-fashioned brick-and-mortar architecture, a two-story frame, and an aging placard that read AJ DIAGNOSTICS. Once inside, Charlie found his office without much effort. It was a retro affair, complete with faux wooden walls, shag carpeting the color of burnt umber, and a steel desk right out of a 1930s-era school principal's office. Seated at the desk was a weathered-looking man, sixty-five, perhaps seventy in years, clad in a denim shirt, faded khakis, and a Red Sox baseball cap.

Charlie knocked once. "Excuse me. Alfred Jenkins?"

He looked up and, in a voice as rocky as the hills and pits on his face, said, "You're looking at him." He ambled toward Charlie, offering his hand. Jenkins got close enough for Charlie to catch a whiff of tobacco. Maybe this was someone who could actually offer him something, someone who could cut through all the bullshit.

"I'm Charlie Redmond."

"Yep, I know. Al's fine. Dougherty told me you were coming. He couldn't have been more excited to set up our meeting. Squirrely bastard. Have a seat."

"Okay," Jenkins said, once they'd settled, "Carla hired you to find Lyle's killer."

"In a nutshell, yes."

"Well, I hate to be the bearer of bad news here, but nobody in this room is responsible. Heck, nobody else who works here is responsible. For starters, access to Lyle wasn't easy from outside the hallowed halls of his company. I incorporated my little company about five years after Lyle started his flagship office a few blocks down the road from here, and I know most of the people who've ever worked there.

"Sure, there were employees who vied for the chance to get products to either be sanctioned by Lyle or to be placed on a development team with him. But I don't see how anyone could or would want him dead. People looked up to him too much. The police were snooping around after his murder, asking questions about his possible infidelity and such because he was at work at all hours, trying to smear his name and create all sorts of angles. Just ridiculous!

"His work ethic demanded commitment. If that meant keeping weird hours, grabbing a good stiff drink whenever the hell he wanted, and being surrounded by talented employees who just happened to be a shit-load of hot broads, then so be it! Shit, if he wanted to bang some power-hungry bitch in the broom closet, he could have done it. I suppose if he pissed off the wrong female she could have offed him, but I really doubt that happened."

"Why's that?" Charlie questioned, bristling at the crudeness of Jenkins's words.

"This facet of the medical device business, the product development and preproduction phase, requires those working within it to eat, breathe, and, yes, sometimes sleep, together. Platonically, of course, until crucial phases of the rollout begin. Those fortunate enough to work with someone of Lyle's caliber knew all of that before going in. And they accepted whatever burdens that job entailed. So, if the head honcho was tight sexu-ally with anyone, it wouldn't take long for anyone else to find out about it." Jenkins smiled and said, "You know how to tell if two people are banging each other in this environment?"

Charlie shrugged.

"Well, they just don't communicate with each other on the job. Easier that way. Wam, bam, thank you, ma'am . . . or sir, depending upon one's inclinations."

"Sounds like they acted like a bunch of horny col-lege students."

"Awww, man. Shit happens all the time here and at a company like Lyle's. Even more so at a place like MedTec. The more successful the company, the better. Actually, the more frisky and bold the employee, the more productive they are. It's kinda weird. It's like those behaviors feed off each other. It's also one of the reasons

I got into this business. During down periods, it can be rather boring around places like this. But during boom times . . . look the hell out! If Lyle were having an affair, he wouldn't be having it within the confines of MedTec. He sure as hell never had that kind of fun at work."

"Okay, what about outside of work?"

"Not as familiar with whomever he socialized with outside of his job. No one from my company, that's for sure."

"Did he hang out with establishment types—politicos and the like?"

"Well, now that you mention it, Lyle was kind of a strange bird. He desired, almost craved, young blood in both social and work settings. But outside, he was much more discriminating. When he first opened his flagship office, he sought out the types of relationships that would net him the most capital and support for his company's infrastructure."

"Oh, so, Mr. Willems knew to play the field for investors, those with deep pockets and innovative spirits."

"Something like that, yes," said Jenkins. "The venture capitalist in him sought promising startup companies that shared his creative vision. Lyle was one of the few CEOs able to lend a helping fiscal hand to many companies bruised by the dot-com bust years ago. Lyle caught the attention of Old Money and liberal politicos who shared his passion for discovery. It may have appeared to others that Lyle was trying to make high-society power plays, but Lyle kept it real. He knew where his bread was buttered."

"The country club crowd?"

"Well, that kind of thing suited his wife more than him. Status was much more important to her."

"Sure," Charlie said. "Totally understand. I've known women who felt the same way. So, did Lyle Willems love his second wife, Emily?"

"I really don't know for sure. I'm sure she filled a void after the death of his first wife. But appearances mean a lot, too."

"How do you mean?"

"Lyle got married within three months of the plane crash that killed his first wife. In public, he appeared to cherish Emily. They were always seen together. But, the Lyle I knew could also be a skillful manipulator. He was successful for a reason. Yeah, it was kinda strange that he was able to rebound so quickly after his first wife's death. But that was Lyle. If the method to his madness was to have a wife on one arm and his high-falutin socialite lifestyle on the other, it wasn't outside the realm of possibility that he would do whatever he could to create and maintain that coexistence. It served a couple of purposes. One, having a wife kept him relevant. It made him real and human. Others would continue to look up to him and his resilience after tragedy. And two, it brought him constant success. Everyone wanted to contribute to him, to work for him, and to celebrate him.

"The longer he could keep up such a lifestyle, the better. Creative types like Lyle got to be where they were by making sure everything behind the scenes perfectly clicked together to present the perfect picture of themselves before the world. It was like a means to all the loose ends he would shore up. Did he piss some people off in the process? I hope not, but with Lyle, you never really knew. The only one who knew him that well was himself. I'm pretty sure Emily just accepted that part. His lifestyle was too important to her. That Lyle, crazy like a fox."

Charlie liked Alfred Jenkins, in spite of his brusqueness. He felt he almost knew Lyle as well as Jenkins did, as a result. There was nothing else he thought he could ask him at this point, except for one question.

"So, Al" Charlie said, "who should I talk to now?"

"Don't know. No one really seems to know much of anything. Guess that's why the case is on ice." Jenkins paused and grinned. "I'm sure that's why Portsmouth's Finest brought you in."

Charlie ignored the comment. "I'm wondering if Emily has much to tell."

"Doubt it," Jenkins said. "But I'll say that she didn't like all the undue attention her husband's unfortunate demise brought. Ordinarily, she's a fiercely private person. She could be hard for an official investigator type like you to read."

"I always benefit from talking with people who knew the victim," Charlie said. "Much like we're doing now. Right, Al? Even if you don't get much from them in the beginning, things have a way of coming to light as time goes on."

"Well, I don't want you to wait for useful information from me. I want to give it to you now. I just thought of one name, though. Larry Ash. He's a two-bit advertising hack with an office not far from me. People are saying if anyone could have done Lyle in, it would have been this guy."

"I've come across his name."

"Larry runs an ad agency. Instant Fame, it's called. Used to be Ashton Advertising. He and his crappy operation are so consumed with competition, I wouldn't put it past him to do whatever he could to land an account by getting Lyle out of the way. One account from MedTec is worth hundreds of accounts from other smaller device companies . . . like mine. Amazing he hasn't run that place into the ground, what with his supposed blow habit and all."

"Cocaine?" Charlie asked, not concealing his surprise. "How do you know about that?"

"Portsmouth isn't that big. You know that, Charlie. Rumor and innuendo fly in this town all the time. Heck, could be bullshit, for all I know. But since when's that stopped anyone from sayin' whatever they want to bring somebody down? Just keep that in mind while you're checkin' things out about Lyle."

Charlie shook his head and chuckled in mild disbelief.

"What's so funny?" Jenkins demanded. "Hell, drugs are probably how Larry was crazy enough to have the balls to weave his slimy self into MedTec meetings."

Charlie kept at it with Jenkins, until the important talk became just small talk. On his way out of Jenkins's company, he couldn't believe he left out one particular query. "Al, how are things here? Are you getting by?"

"We're still open for business, aren't we?" Jenkins laughed. "I'm nowhere near as prolific in my output as Lyle was, nowhere as polished, but I can hold my own. . . .Yep, mostly, all I do is make sure things here don't go to shit. I've got a pretty dedicated group of developers.

They're a small bunch, but hardworking. Bills get paid. Things keep on keepin' on."

"I'm sure Lyle would have appreciated that," Charlie said, once again appreciative of Jenkins's plainspokenness.

"Yeah," Jenkins said with a sheepish grin.

Charlie smiled to himself. He had more critical information about Lyle. He'd found out his values, his work ethic, and his likes and dislikes. He was beginning to understand what made Lyle tick. But Charlie knew that he was miles from figuring out a motive for Lyle Willems's murder. Maybe going back to Dougherty would yield some answers.

CHAPTER 10

When Charlie raised his arm to knock on Dougherty's office, Dougherty opened the door first, almost running into Charlie in the process. Charlie motioned as though he were going into the office, but Dougherty didn't budge.

"Oh," said Charlie, "it was my understanding I was going to interview you. I wanted to make sure of it before heading back to my place for a run."

"Well, I was thinking we'd go out for a coffee, or a beer," Dougherty said, firmly but politely.

Shit, the unintended hazards of this job.

"Um, sure. I guess I can run tomorrow morning."

"Of course. You can go for a run anytime. Heck, you've got a pretty athletic frame. I'm sure you could afford not to run and just take it easy from time to time. Come on, it'll be good for you to unwind. Change of scenery and all that. Plus, I have a joint."

Charlie wondered if Ken were patronizing him or admiring him. "You're assuming I do pot?" Charlie asked.

"Yes."

"Ken, I haven't done this shit since college. You know, you're a bad influence on a retired police detective trying to do his job," Charlie said, recalling the substance that fueled his halcyon days as an undergraduate. He smiled, and immediately relented.

There are some things Carla doesn't have to know.

"I mean, I used to do it. A long, long time ago. Good times."

"Cool beans!" Dougherty said. "Why don't we go to The Happy Chimp?"

"I'll see you there."

***

The bar was dank and grimy, illuminated only by small scented tabletop candles. The perfect place for Dougherty, who was a few beers and two joints into what he considered the interview, to begin opening up.

"Jeez, I was really, really in a funk for such a long time. Still am. But, you know, it's been over a year and a half since, and I'm still in shock. I'm at a loss as to why. It'd be cool to know the how and why behind Lyle's murder. I'm just really curious, you know? I mean, who hated Lyle enough to freaking kill him, to carve out his neck?"

"I believe you told me that you really never saw him that much outside of the workplace."

"Well, no one really did, you know? Lyle and his wife were uppity society types here in Portsmouth."

"Alfred Jenkins told me that Lyle really hung around with the establishment, old-money type of crowd."

"Yeah, I know," Dougherty said. "Lyle definitely wasn't of that pedigree. But he played along. He charmed and sucked up to the right people the entire way. He was good at it. Bankers. High-profile politicians. Well-funded venture capitalists. You name it. But, I knew Lyle because of his work ethic. Man, he was at the office all the time. So, I found myself around him all the time, as well. He never invited me to hang with him at his social 'power functions,' but when you find yourself around someone that much, you really do get a good idea of their soul. And I really liked Lyle Willems. He had it all— charm, brains, resources, influence. And he was quite the looker—to the ladies, of course."

Dougherty and Charlie snickered, and ordered another round.

"Tell me about this guy Lawrence—I mean, Larry—Ash. Everyone seems to have an opinion about him."

"God, what a fraud. Wait, I was . . . that may have been a little too strong. Larry Ash is a poseur. A charlatan. I honestly don't know how he's been able to last as long as he has in his business and not be run out of town. Oh, and he's a junkie, too. At least, that's what people say about him. I think that if he were somehow responsible for getting Lyle out of commission, he could have engineered things in such a way that he could grab a lot of his lucrative accounts in the company."

Charlie and Dougherty remained at the bar for at least a couple of hours. Talk of Lyle Willems fueled much of the conversation, but the two rambled on about other matters, too. Things like. . . life and the big picture.

The two men maintained empty gazes at each other. The pot must have been doing the talking now. Charlie stared at the runt of a man in front of him. He was disheveled in a nerdy way, with his tight plaid shirt, sweaty round face, comb-over, and silly-ass grin. He hoped that Dougherty wasn't . . . checking him out. The beers and the joints were clouding Charlie's judgment.

Snapping out of his buzz trip, Charlie asked, "Did you ever notice anything off-kilter about Lyle?"

"How so?"

"Okay, what I mean is, was there anything—did you ever see anything about him, what he did—that came across to you as odd? I know that he had some less than ethical proclivities he justified in the name of his company's success. But, did you ever have an instance, in which you thought, well, that's weird, even for Lyle? I mean, it could be *anything*, no matter how inconsequential."

Dougherty struggled to focus. "Well, yes, and no," he began. "One day I arrived at work at little early."

"Was Brian Gardner already there?"

"Who? Oh yeah, Brian. No, but I know what you mean. What a kiss-ass. Anyway, I saw that Lyle was in his office sleeping at his desk. I noticed that he was still in his clothes from the day before. All of a sudden, he woke up, as I walked toward his office."

"Had Lyle been sleeping there, as far as you know?"

"I suppose. Not sure. It's no secret that those who worked at MedTec had a strong work ethic. We worked hard, and we worked a lot. But we always knew when to recharge and call it a day. Lyle knew this and subscribed to this belief, too. But he also was a workaholic, so it's anybody's guess as to the circumstances surrounding that day I saw him there."

Charlie guessed that perhaps Lyle did leave the office, but didn't actually go home. He could have immediately come back to the office to make it appear as though he'd spent the night. He opted not to mention this to Dougherty.

"Ken," Charlie said, "I think we should call a cab, and come back and get our cars tomorrow."

Dougherty stared at him, making him feel a little uncomfortable. His eyes narrowed a bit. "You know, friend, I don't freely talk like this to just anyone. I just want you to know that, Charlie."

Friend?

"Hey, Ken, bud. Thanks, okay? But I think it's time to head home and sleep all this off. I'll call a cab. Just stay there."

Charlie got up from the table, tempted to just walk straight out of the bar. But he held his end of the deal, and a few minutes later he and Dougherty shared an uneasy cab ride home.

CHAPTER 11

C harlie called a cab the next morning and retrieved his car, anxious to call Dougherty and set the record straight about the night before. He wanted to tell Dougherty that whatever he thought was going on between them was a figment of his imagination, or a product of some good substances—or both, for that matter. That the relationship was purely professional because a focused investigator such as himself had to do whatever he could to get the information he needed to crack the case. That any bonding, as a by-product of obtaining said information, was coincidental and could jeopardize future acquisition of potentially useful information.

God, I'm starting to sound like my divorce attorney.

He slapped himself, got out of the cab, and walked toward his Lincoln.

"Hey, Charlie!" Dougherty shouted from across the bar parking lot.

"Hello, Ken," Charlie waved.

"Hey, Charlie. Good to see you this morning. Always good to see—"

"Say, look, Ken. About last night, I just want to you know . . ."

"Say no more. I realize I was a little forward with everything. All you wanted to do was your job and ask

55

me a few questions. Instead, I forced you to go to a bar you probably didn't like for beer that was probably too warm and joints that were a little too potent." Dougherty gave a wry, self-deprecating smile before saying, "I should have stayed professional. Because, after all, you are acting professionally, each and every time you ask questions that have to do with a case. I used you, and, for that, I apologize."

Charlie wanted to tell him that the pot was the best part, but he was interrupted by a text on his cell phone. It was from Carla.

My mother's agreed to meet with you—today.

"Damn. Sorry, Ken I have to get this," Charlie said. The goddamn text couldn't have come at a worse time! He apologized to Dougherty before hopping back into his Lincoln.

Back at the bungalow, Charlie skipped the morning's *New York Times*, gulped two large mugs of black coffee, and then jumped on the phone with Emily Willems, who answered on the first ring. After introducing himself, Charlie asked if now was a good time to speak about her late husband.

"Yes," she said, her voice just a little more subdued, "Carla said you'd be calling now. Is this not a good time for you?"

Charlie knew what anxiety sounded like. Textbook case.

"Yes, yes…absolutely, I can talk now. You sound a little tired. I can call later if—"

"No," she answered. "I'm okay. I mean, I'm fine, go ahead."

"If you're able, I'd like to ask you about your late husband."

"I think I've been very forthcoming with the police already. You can talk with them, can't you?"

"Well, sure," Charlie said, a little startled by her reticence. "But I think it would help me more to talk with you."

"So you can conclude that I had something to do with all this?"

"Well, no, Emily," Charlie said cautiously. "I need to determine whether or not you had anything, anything at all, to do with it. And, by extension, help me to determine who did have something to do with it. If you didn't, of course."

There was a pause on the other end. "It's 'Mrs. Willems,'" Emily said. "That's what the other detectives called me."

Charlie felt pink creep into his cheeks. She continued, saving Charlie from saying anything off-color. "I really don't want to come off as impertinent, Detective. I mean, I just know you're doing your job, but we're all finally putting this whole awful episode behind us. It is extremely painful to have a loved one, a spouse killed. You may or may not realize this, but you get to a point where you're just numb to the entire thing. You just want it to end."

Funny . . . her daughter feels exactly the opposite.

"I understand, but I'd really like to.

Talk with you in person, will you speak with me?"

"Well . . . I suppose I can."

Charlie let loose the faintest of sighs under his breath. "Great," he said. "I can come by tomorrow afternoon."

She said, "For your information, the other detectives always referred to me as Mrs. Willems."

Damn, this woman is insistent.

"Is that what you want me to call you?"

"I'm just wondering why you didn't."

"Okay, let's review. Emily's your name, correct?"

"Yes."

"That's why I didn't. Problem solved. See you tomorrow."

Charlie hung up with Emily, and wondered why he hadn't heard back yet from Lawrence Ash, the advertising executive. It was a sweet score. Charlie was able to persuade Emily Willems to talk to him, but he hadn't yet heard back from Ash. He'd called him three times. Even spoke with his executive assistant, Darlene, but had no confirmation from her about meeting with her boss, not even a callback.

Charlie decided to place a call to his detective friend Steve Richards, who was there to pick up. The best way to get him to open up would be to invite him for pizza at Luigi's—a hole-in-the-wall joint they both loved. When Charlie made it to the restaurant, he discovered that Richards had beaten him there.

"Charlie, my good man. How are you today? Didn't expect the Great One to be crawling back to me so soon for help."

Charlie disregarded the remark, and the two sat down in a rear booth Richards had chosen.

Charlie loved Luigi's. It was the worst place to chow down on hole-in-the-wall Italian if you were in training. But its authentic scents, carb heavy menu, and ambiance were perfect comforts for earnest, intensive discussion.

It was just the beginning of the lunch hour, and already Charlie was craving empty calories in the form of a cold beer. He ordered a Bud Light. Richards had one too, so apparently he wasn't on duty. They placed their orders and got to the matter at hand, Lawrence Ash.

"I did some digging into Lawrence Ash, or Larry for short," said Richards. "That's what everyone calls him. Doesn't look like the nicest guy in the world."

"No surprise there," Charlie said. "Like I said, Steve, at least three calls and messages to this guy, and no returns."

"Charlie, you probably know from the police reports that Larry Ash was only referred to as a person of interest. The two detectives who interviewed him declined to pursue things further after what looked like to me pretty intense questioning."

"Who are those two detectives?"

"Ray Lewis and Tom Liedeman. I told them that you were reopening the case. Of course, you're free to contact them if you'd like."

"Yeah, sure."

"Let's see," Richards said, shuffling through documents and spilling beer on a couple of sheets. "Sorry. Looks like Liedeman was transferred to Portland, Maine."

"Why was that?" asked Charlie.

"Pretty weird. Detectives don't transfer often."

"Yeah, practically never."

"Won't he have to work his way back up? And why Portland?"

"Well, I thought so, too. But Liedeman knows the captain up there. He was basically able to slide in with the same benefits, but a higher salary. Anything helps, I suppose. You know, we don't make bank like you detective-turned-PI guys. You guys get to charge whatever the fuck you want. Think I'm in the wrong biz."

Charlie wanted to correct his former colleague's nonsensical assertions, but figured it was a lost cause.

Richards said, "Detective Lewis reported that Larry Ash was extremely jealous of Lyle Willems."

"Yeah, Ash runs an ad agency not far from Lyle Willems's place. Basically, he would try to obtain medical device accounts from Lyle's company that had the potential to sell through the roof. Always seemed to wear out his welcome there."

"Right," Richards said. "Everyone questioned thought Ash may have been obsessed with Lyle Willems."

"In addition," Charlie replied, "it doesn't matter what Ash does, the rest of the advertising world, locally at least, always points the finger at him, assuming he'll do whatever he can to sabotage other agencies."

Their pepperoni slices arrived, and Richards took a bite. "No one could get any info on him, though. But you already know that, don't you? But, the detectives didn't know then what I'm about to tell you now. That's because what I'm about to tell you hadn't happened yet. And it has nothing to do with Lyle Willems."

Charlie held up his right hand. His left hand held a slice of pepperoni. "Before you give me this information, let me tell you my inclinations and thoughts. Ash talked to the cops at the time, was very cooperative then, right?"

"You read the report. They way they questioned him was grueling."

"Well, in all the messages I left for Ash, I never told him why I was calling. So, I'm guessing he doesn't think that I'm calling about that. That's because, even if he is hiding information on Lyle Willems, he already knows what he'll say regarding his murder. He really has no reason to avoid me. He didn't avoid the police. So, why would he avoid me? I think he's concerned about something else."

"The Great One emerges," Richards grinned.

Charlie continued, "I think that, if he's worried about something else, perhaps I can sort of confuse him into telling me something about Lyle Willems before he catches on to my strategy and—"

Richards put up a hand. "Let me tell you what I know, first."

"Okay."

"Here's the deal. Guy's been in and out of rehab. So, word's out he's into drugs. Could be a touch of mental instability going on, too."

"Okay."

Richards lowered his voice. "Larry Ash was behind a major investment in a company run by a guy named Vincent Contadino. It's a durable medical equipment company. You know, the companies that produce things like wheelchairs and oxygen tanks. Company's name is Rockland. Rockland Medical Supply."

"Hmmm. Never heard of this character."

"Well, the department is long familiar with him. We know he's deep into organized crime."

"How deep?"

"As deep as he can be. He runs it all."

The waitress coming up behind Charlie's shoulder met Steve Richards's glare. She retreated just as quickly, saying "Oh, I'll come back in a few."

"Family involved?"

"As far as we know, not. He just runs it. He's at the very top. But, of course, we've always had trouble catching him at his dealings. Can't prove shit on him. But that's another story for another day," Richards said.

"And the company, legit or a front of some kind?"

"It's legit, for the most part. Problem is, the way his company acquires business is bullshit. Contadino has tentacles into many manufacturers in New England, particularly along southern coastal Maine, southern New Hampshire, and coastal Mass. He knows 'em all. Turns out, mob ties are responsible for funneling all that business to his company, which, it follows, is extremely successful.

"All his employees think that they're just fortunate to work for one of the most successful medical equipment companies in the region. Sure, Contadino knows there are other companies that bid for contracts, but Rockland has a particularly prosperous way of obtaining business."

"Do you have any intel into Larry Ash's knowledge of Contadino's level of involvement?"

"I don't, really. But, I couldn't care less. You see, Ash is just a stooge. Contadino approached him with a business deal that he just couldn't refuse. It was probably a win-win for him. You run into Contadino, now, there's a scary motherfucker. He exudes fear. I'd bet dollars to doughnuts Ash knows it, too. He may even know the score, for all I know. I think that your having this information could rattle him a bit. Advance your cause, so to speak."

"All right, let me ask you this," said Charlie. "Just how scary is this Contadino? How shaken would Larry Ash be if he thought that he pissed Contadino off in some way?"

"Very," said Richards. "I know that I said he had tentacles all over the region. But, he's no octopus. People refer to him as 'Contadino the Shark.' That phrase describes how he conducts business and how he kills—without remorse."

Charlie stared at Richards.

"What the fuck is it now?" Richards said.

"You mean to tell me you're just giving me this confidential info, no strings attached? Hold on, I'll take a stab at this. Some of the muckety-mucks at the station are probably involved in all this bullshit and are basically getting in the way of busting this guy. And you're pretty pissed off about it."

"Your words. Not mine."

"Don't know what to say, Steve," Charlie said. Richards didn't answer. Instead he just got up from the booth and left.

Charlie watched as his buddy left the restaurant. He knew that the existence of a cold case—any cold case—irritated Richards. He wanted them solved—the first time. Charlie wished he could've ended the conversation on a more positive note, because he suddenly realized that Richards was in his corner. If his egotism got in the way of telling Charlie just how much he believed in his skills, well, that was just Steve Richards, Charlie thought. He never would tell Charlie to his face how much he needed him to solve Lyle Willems's murder. Richards was just glad he agreed to do it. Charlie smiled. He wasn't going to let his buddy down.

CHAPTER 12

Charlie returned to his bungalow from a ten-mile run the next morning, to find his cell phone ringing. Darlene, Lawrence Ash's assistant, apologized for taking several days to call back. She asked if Charlie could meet the next morning at nine at Instant Fame.

"Perfect. I'll be there," he said, figuring it'd do no good to fly off the handle.

"Good," she said. "Lawrence looks forward to seeing you then."

***

The next day, at ten before nine, Charlie pulled up to a nondescript three-story brick building. He found the reception area littered with copies of an industry-related advertising magazine, with Lawrence Ash on the cover. Below Lawrence's blue knit shirt, chino pants, and tinted sunglasses was the headline: INSTANT FAME ISN'T FLEETING FOR LARRY ASH.

Charlie searched the magazine for the article. Apparently six years earlier, Ash had been plodding along as an average copywriter at a small agency in Boston when a very close female friend married a man named Will Sterling—the seventy-year-old founder and creative director of Instant Fame, an ad agency based in suburban Boston. Sterling soon retired and made Larry Ash the new owner. Good-bye Ashton Advertising.

Ash immediately moved the operation to Portsmouth, and changed the focus of the company from insurance and department store accounts to the red-hot medical device market. The article questioned the wisdom of his choices, and whether he could have reached such heights on his own merits.

Charlie wondered why so many copies were out in the open, when a stunning brunette appeared. He took a moment to subtly appreciate her smart beige pants, vanilla blouse, and lovely white smile. "I'm Darlene, Larry's assistant," she said.

"Charlie. It's really good to meet you."

"Larry's ready to see you now. Why don't you follow me?"

Charlie looked around as they entered the agency. Familiar prints of best-selling medical devices covered the walls.

Pretty odd. Then, he realized: the images were of products that MedTec had created, all of them. For an agency yet to land an account with a medical device company that had all but shunned it, Ash was either in serious denial, or was just plain oblivious to his managerial shortcomings.

They took the elevator to the second floor, where a centrally located office looked eerily similar to Lyle Willems's, right down to the hexagonal glass enclosure, desk, and singular bookshelf directly across the room.

"Well, here we are," said Darlene.

Charlie looked in the office and saw Larry Ash wearing practically the same outfit as the one in the magazine, with the same sunglasses, too. This time, they rested on the bridge of his nose. Ash motioned to Charlie and Darlene he'd get off his call momentarily.

Darlene left to go back to her desk, just outside Ash's office. Ash hung up his office phone and walked toward the door, but not before putting up his hand, indicating Charlie to hold on a minute. He walked around to the other side of his desk, adjacent to his leather chair, and knelt behind the desk.

Weird.

Ash finally walked toward Charlie and stuck out his right hand.

"Larry Ash," he said. "Why don't we have a seat?"

The two men sat down across from each other. "Darlene showed you around some? You like our offices here?" asked Ash, flashing a cocky smile.

How 'bout you take your sunglasses off so I could see your face? Oh, that's right: the future's so bright you have to wear shades.

"Actually, this building reminds me of MedTec headquarters," Charlie said.

"Yeah, but I do strive to maintain my own identity." Ash winked his right eye, smiled, and took a long sniff through his nose.

You must have found what you were looking for underneath your desk.

"I make no secrets about how much I desire one or more of MedTec's accounts," Ash continued. "The pictures on the first floor merely represent the respect I've always held for Lyle Willems. May he rest in peace. I'm not the only ad guy in the area who feels that way. He is truly missed."

Charlie stared in his direction, unblinking.

"So what's this all about?" asked Ash. "Of course, I know, why am I asking? It's that Lyle Willems case from over a year ago. Right?"

"Year and a half—almost two, to be exact, but we can talk about that, sure."

"Dude, I've already talked to the cops out the ass. I don't have anything more to say. If you don't believe me, just look at the police reports. Detectives like you do that, right?"

"What exactly was your relationship to Mr. Willems?" Charlie asked, evenly.

"Look, I'm a busy guy," said Ash. Charlie marveled at Ash's immature, erratic, and impetuous behavior. He wondered how this guy was able to get out of bed every morning, much less run a major advertising agency.

Holy crap, this guy is climbing the walls. How the hell does he get the blow from in his desk?

"All right," Ash said. "I'm extremely busy, as you've probably gathered. I'm in charge of an ad agency that's worth over two hundred million dollars. Why don't you just talk to his wife? I heard that he was unfaithful while he was married to her. He used to cheat on her. That's what I heard, anyway."

"I will be talking with Ms. Willems, his widow. But now, I'm talking to you."

"I have nothing else to say on this topic, capice?"

Charlie looked through Ash's dark sunglasses as though they were crystal clear, and said, "Then let's talk about another topic. Larry, do you do any investing on your own?"

Charlie detected a flash of emotion on Ash's face.

"Yeah, I dabble. It's how I make money." Ash promptly switched topics. "Okay, what do you want to know about Lyle Willems? I really don't see how much more I can give you, but I'll indulge you."

"What was your relationship to him?"

"Although we worked in different facets of product development, we were competitors."

"Would you say you were equals?"

"Of course not," Ash said. He shifted in his leather chair. "Lyle Willems was truly a legend. He had no equal."

"Did you secretly infiltrate product preproduction meetings without Mr. Willems's knowledge?"

"No, and none of my employees would say that. When I consulted with Lyle, it was always the result of a mutual arrangement. If MedTec didn't want me there, I didn't go."

"Well, I've heard otherwise. From various MedTec employees."

"Well, I think they're leading you astray. They would say anything to slander my company, to bring me down. But I'm still here. It's called competition. Get used to it."

Charlie noticed perspiration forming above Ash's sunglasses. "So what kind of investments do you have? Other companies?"

Ash didn't answer. He looked down at the floor, then above Charlie's head, then at the bookshelf.

"Larry?" Charlie said.

"All sorts of things. I play the market. I invest in my company. I invest—"

"Would you say that the ad biz is a cutthroat one?"

"What are you here to ask me about?"

"Lyle Willems," Charlie said.

"Sure, sure. Yes, I would say advertising is a cutthroat business."

"Would you say cutthroat enough to kill someone over accounts, money, inside information?"

"I really don't know what you're implying," Ash said, returning to the mojo he had when Charlie started the interview.

"I'm asking you a question," Charlie said. "Is that sort of thing cutthroat?"

"Well, I know that *I* wouldn't say that.

Look around you, Detective, this company does quite well with the current accounts we have. Quite well. Instant Fame excels based upon its own merits, not by unethical, illegal actions." Larry sniffed.

"So, when you earn an account—rather, win one—do you have to get to know the owner of that company?"

"Of course, if it's a private company. They're giving us their business."

"So, you have relationships with many owners."

"Yeah, of course."

"Do you personally know the owners of businesses you don't do ads for?"

"What's this about? Are we still talking about Lyle Willems?"

"We can talk about that," Charlie said. "Like I already told you."

"So ask me a question about Lyle Willems." Ash's eyes shifted back and forth.

"Hold on. Give me the name of a company owner you know but don't have accounts with."

"Why?"

"Why not?"

"What's this got to do with Lyle Willems?" Ash asked.

"You tell me."

"What?"

Charlie enjoyed taking Ash on a ride, but he knew that the possibility of obtaining any information of value at this visit was as fleeting as Ash's train of thought.

This guy is on a roller coaster going a million miles an hour. Have to get off.

"I gotta run, Larry. Thanks for finally getting around to seeing me," Charlie said.

"You mean, we're done?"

"Do you have something else to tell me?"

Larry Ash rose from his leather chair. Charlie also stood. He pulled out a business card and threw it on Ash's desk. "If you have anything you want to tell me, just call or e-mail."

"Detective … Charlie," Ash said. Charlie stopped and turned.

"Why were you asking me all those questions about my investments and all that bullshit?"

"Why do you think?"

"No idea. That's why I asked."

"Larry, that's what we investigators do. We try to connect all the things about the case we're investigating, or about a person, and try to solve the bigger puzzle." Charlie paused and realized he'd have to obtain information from Ash with more deliberate planning. He'd screwed with Ash enough, but he couldn't resist one last jab before concluding the interview.

"Larry, where are you from? Where'd you grow up?"

"Boston," Ash said.

"Good to know," Charlie said. He turned around and walked out.

***

Outside, as Charlie got in his Lincoln, someone called his name. It was Darlene, Larry Ash's assistant. Charlie was distracted by her sexy form as she ran toward him.

"Hey. Glad I caught up with you," she said.

"Yeah."

"Stand right there. I want to get a good look at you."

Charlie didn't know what to make of Darlene's request, but he played along.

"Now, move over to your right a little. Sun's in my eyes."

Charlie obliged.

"Okay, stop." Darlene paused. "Yep, it's you, all right."

"All right," Charlie said, rolling his eyes, "I give up. What are you doing?"

"Kinky Bastards," Darlene said.

Charlie stared at her.

"Kinky Bastards," Darlene said, as if daring him to respond. She smiled mischievously.

Nausea built in Charlie's stomach.

Oh my God. She knows. How the hell does this woman know about that? Fuck me, that was, shit, years ago. Holy Christ.

"Oh boy, looks like I triggered a neuron."

"H-How . . . How did you know?"

"Hey. You okay, Charlie? Can I call you that? It's okay. I really don't care. Personally, I think it's hot."

Charlie knew right at that moment, that any possibility of Darlene taking him seriously would probably be lost forever. He looked down at his feet. "I . . . I don't know what to say."

"Hey, hey. It's okay. Really." Darlene motioned him to her minivan. "Here, follow me. Let's go sit."

Darlene sat in the driver's seat. "I just want to tell you," she continued, "the only reason I know about Kinky Bastards is because I submitted a video, too." She looked in his eyes while she rubbed his left shoulder in support.

My God, I thought that part of my life was buried forever.

"Look, it was ten years ago," Darlene said, "around the time you and whoever you were with at the time also had a video up on that site. I was so young, stupid, and immature. At the time, it seemed like the right thing to do. And getting paid for it was the best part. The money my boyfriend and I made back then really, really helped."

Charlie had to come clean. Had to be honest with her. After all, he expected people to be honest with him.

"My ex put me up to it," he said. "I should have seen the warning signs back then. She said she wanted more spice in the relationship. Said she didn't feel like a true partner in marriage. And putting a homemade porno up on that stupid-ass website seemed, well . . . seemed appropriate."

Charlie had gone through with it. There was no immediate fallout, except for the humiliation. Actually, the only problem he had with doing something like that was that it didn't have the eventual effect either of them desired. Their sex life didn't improve, and they grew further apart. Charlie calling her a faker didn't help things, he recalled. All in all, the experiment was a massive fail.

"I'm sorry," Charlie continued. "We actually grew further apart as a result of it."

"It's okay. Really," Darlene reassured him. "We do what we have to do at the time."

Minutes passed. To Charlie, it seemed like eons.

"Yeah," he said, looking out at the parking lot.

"Listen, Charlie, take my card. If I can ever help you . . . getting in touch with Larry, or whatever, please, get in touch with me."

She handed Charlie her business card. It read "DARLENE CONNOLLY, ADVISER, INSTANT FAME."

Adviser, huh? Wonder if she could advise me out of the creative funk I'm in, both sexually and professionally.

"Thanks, Darlene."

"Well, how 'bout giving me *your* card?"

He handed Darlene one of his old cards, the same type he'd given to both Ash and Carla Willems.

"You know, we don't have to talk about Larry," Darlene said. "We could, um, I don't know, have a drink, or whatever."

Charlie turned toward Darlene before looking out again at the parking lot. He put on shades he pulled from his left breast pocket. "I think we could set that up," he said.

Darlene smiled at him. He forgot about feeling nauseated. Then, before he could restrain himself, he said, "You know, I'm probably at least ten, fifteen years older

74

than you." He wasn't sure why he said it. Wish it hadn't left his lips. It sounded forced and senseless.

"So?" she said.

Exactly.

"You make a good point," Charlie said.

She smiled. "I can see myself in the reflection of your sunglasses. I look silly. They certainly suit you better than Larry. He looks like some low-rent porn star."

Wow, I have a word for how you look.

"Well, okay, bye, Charlie. It was nice to meet you," said Darlene, awkwardly.

"Nice to meet you, too."

Yes, very nice.

They got out of the minivan, and she started for the entrance of Instant Fame. He stood there, ogling her brunette hair bob up and down in unison with her firm posterior, wrapped in that smart beige blouse. He watched her disappear behind a row of service vans. Any shame Charlie had in previous actions with his ex disappeared after he met Darlene. She made him feel that it was okay to experiment and make mistakes, and to move on if goals weren't achieved.

She's exciting. And she understands me. But, she's moving a little fast. But still ... that body. . . .

He nodded and said out loud to no one in particular, "She's got it goin' on." A little embarrassed, Charlie turned around and walked toward the Lincoln.

***

Charlie arrived home, straightened up the bangalow, walked Thompson, and thought about things. He had picked up some new gear meant for his trip to New Zealand and decided to try out the new ultra light sweat-wicking running shorts and performance running shoes on a run. Five miles today, he told himself. After the run, he walked toward the shore of the Piscataqua. The sun gradually slipped behind the horizon. Charlie walked a bit. Alone time. Time to think. He stewed over Ash. Larry Ash, a stooge and poseur, definitely an asshole—and probably a liar. His investments were questionable, at the very least, but was he a murderer? If he was, what was his motive? Who knows? You have to be cunning or manipulative to kill someone. Experience told him it was quite the opposite. A power hungry, obsessed drug addict could kill, might kill. But what was the motivation? Was it to get more business, to take out the biggest player in the game? Did he have any other sort of relationship with Lyle Willems? According to the phone records, the two never spoke over the phone. It was always in person, and very rare, at that.

Ash knows I'm after something, but he's not sure. I'll use that as leverage to achieve my goal. Eventually.

And what about Lyle Willems's late nights? The cops, Jenkins, and even Larry Ash all told the same story. Was he anything more than an unusually gifted, hardworking eccentric? Emily Willems would have to address that tomorrow, that is, if Charlie could get her to talk.

Nightfall. Back at the bungalow, Charlie plopped down on the couch, petted the dog, and grabbed a Bud Light. Just who the hell was Lyle Willems? What was he hiding *or doing* that no one, not even his closest coworkers, had even the slightest knowledge of? What got him murdered? There was no time for answers, as Charlie, feeling exhausted but renewed, fell asleep right there on the couch.

CHAPTER 13

The next morning, Charlie pulled up to an estate in Portsmouth's New Castle neighborhood, with a beautiful view of the mouth of the Piscataqua. He remembered that Emily Willems had money before she married Lyle, so it may have been a stretch to assume that Lyle's wealth was solely responsible for the property.

He got out of his car and noticed the mansion was set off from other properties in the immediate area by walls of bulky shrubby and landscaping. The well-manicured perimeter almost dared anyone to stray from the elegant walkways to set foot on it. Charlie didn't stray. It was the least he could do, in deference to Emily Willems.

Charlie rang the doorbell, and overheard dogs barking. The barking didn't sound like the lets-get-ready-to-pounce-on-whomever-it-is-because-this-compound-must-be-guarded-at-all-costs type, just complementing-the-doorbell barks. The front door opened, and Emily Willems stood in the entryway, flanked by a couple of Samoyeds. She wore her hair in an alluring manner, and wore a white pantsuit more suited for giving a luxury home tour than lounging around her home, walking her dogs. She was stately. Exquisitely lean. She wore a nice, elegant necklace. Make that a choker. That's what Charlie felt like doing when she first spoke to him via phone. He perished that thought.

"Twila and Trevor," Emily said as Charlie bent down to pet both animals. "They're Samoyeds. Both were given to me by my son, Guy, a couple of years ago."

Charlie assumed Guy was her biological son, Guy Wright, from the first marriage. Charlie made a mental note to interview him.

"He named them," she said. "Come, Mr. Redmond, shall we sit on the patio?"

Charlie followed Emily Willems through the immaculate, museum-like foyer, which still managed to be warm. Pictures of Lyle covered the walls: Lyle and politicians. Lyle and celebrities. And not just any old celebrities or politicos. It was only the best company for Lyle Willems, A-listers and deep-pocketed Democrats. One of the largest prints, directly adjacent to the entrance to one of the guest rooms on the ground floor, showed a smiling Lyle and former president Bill Clinton. Emily was particularly proud of this one. Charlie wanted to ask if it were the real deal, but his detective skills told him it was.

Status must have mattered to Emily, since there were no pictures, even on the fireplace mantel back in the foyer, that displayed only her and Lyle. If they were pictured together, it was always with someone of stature. Charlie could tell she was green with envy over the Bill Clinton snub. Lyle was no marquee idol, but he exuded his own brand of celebrity looks. He was a businessman who owned the title of chief executive officer. He practically redefined what it meant to be a company CEO. Because of his facility with leadership, the country club set respected him. The political crowd admired him. His employees valued him. Jack Welch,

Lee Iacocca, Sam Walton . . . those were apparently the kind of celebrities Emily adored.

Outside, Emily guided Charlie to a medium-sized four-person stone table on the edge of the patio, where a pitcher of lemonade sat waiting for them. From their vantage, they could see where the mouth of the Piscataqua met the Atlantic. Stunning.

"This thing," she said. "This whole murder thing is so very difficult for me to talk about. Not as much Lyle's death, but thinking about who was responsible for it. That's what hurts."

Emily spoke her words with the same peevish edge as she had previously with Charlie over the phone.

"I completely understand," Charlie said. "Thank you for taking the time to speak with me."

"I think that he's looking down upon us, smiling, now that you're on the case," she said, with equal parts placation and condescension. She couldn't hide the latter very well. Even if she could, Charlie would have sensed it.

Charlie couldn't shake the comment Larry Ash had made earlier, about Emily. *Why don't you talk to his wife? I heard that he was unfaithful while he was married to her. He used to cheat on her. That's what I heard, anyway.* He took a sip of his lemonade. He didn't think that she would ever admit to infidelity on Lyle's part. She was too proud.

"Alfred Jenkins told me that he didn't think anyone at MedTec had it in 'em to kill your husband."

"He's right. I don't think anyone in the industry, advertising or medical devices, killed him."

"Why's that?"

"I know that the environment can be a competitive one. Securing accounts is serious business. Tell me, have you ever gone into an ad agency?"

"Yeah, a couple, or so."

"Those types aren't particularly dangerous. They're all just working stiffs with jobs. The vast majority of them are only in it for the paycheck and benefits right out of college. They're not committed, not like Lyle, anyway. You have to be driven to commit murder. Many in these industries are only in their current situations as stepping-stones. The creative types you've probably already heard so much about in Lyle's company, 95 percent of them, aspire to be novelists, artists, creators of other stripes in places ultimately far more satisfying than their temporary stints at companies like MedTec or Instant Fame. For those who wound up being in Lyle's inner sanctum, or close to it, anyway, it took years for them to reach that level, along with luck and determination. Almost right after Lyle's murder, many expressed an interest in Larry Ash. I'm not sure what he would have gained by killing my husband. It's not like he'd be more likely to obtain any lucrative accounts with MedTec. In fact, he still hasn't. He still has to earn them, win them."

"According to the cops, he was jealous of your husband. Obsessively so."

"Perhaps. Larry's definitely not the most popular man. But even if he were obsessed, it would be difficult to investigate that," she said.

"And this case, as you know, has been cold for quite a while. No strong evidence."

They sipped their lemonade. Charlie thought that it tasted good, homemade. Not that store-bought grit he usually makes at home, his definition of homemade. Made in the home. He paused. "Do you have any theories, Emily?"

"I think the entire thing was random," she said. "An accident. My husband was simply in the wrong place at the wrong time. Someone killed him and physically placed him at the company after the fact to throw everyone off. Of course, it would have been easy to find out who he was and where he worked. I just don't know why anyone would want to do something like this. He didn't do drugs, didn't owe anyone any money. I can't imagine that he had some sort of sinister life about which I knew absolutely nothing."

"You seem to be pretty adamant about this. You're saying he didn't have affairs?"

"That's what I mean. It's why you're here, right? To ask me about this angle, as you detective know-it-alls always put it? Everyone else has asked me the same line of questioning. No, my husband did not have any affairs, Detective. He came home absolutely every single night, unless of course, he was out of town.

"The employees at MedTec like to say he kept these ridiculously outrageous hours and they'd see him having a few drinks somewhere late at night, as if he were this out-of-control alcoholic desperately trying to maintain his lifestyle, profession, and personal life at all costs. Well, you know what? Newsflash. He'd just leave work, wind down, and call me before coming home."

Charlie knew there was at least one night he didn't come home; Ken Dougherty had told him as much. But Emily was defensive, like a rock. She wouldn't have appreciated the public scrutiny an affair would have brought. She was very protective of her and her husband's legacy, if that's what you would call it, and that was understandable, even laudable.

"As you probably know," she continued, "Lyle and I were married later in life. One child. Some people feel you need to have kids to stay together. We didn't have Carla as a necessary crutch. We wanted to have a child. Just wish Carla and I were closer." Emily stopped speaking, her voice cracking.

"But Lyle and I had a wonderful relationship together," she continued. "We loved to talk about movies and plays and business. We had an intellectual relationship. We loved each other very much. He didn't play the field. He didn't run around."

Charlie looked at her, finishing another sip of lemonade. "Let's return to Larry Ash."

"All right," she said, relaxing a bit.

"Why do you think he was questioned so intensely? Sure, he strongly emulated your husband's work ethic. He openly admired him. Was jealous of him, but they rarely talked. No phone records depicting conversations between them were ever authenticated. For all intents and purposes, they had no relationship."

"I'll tell you why, Mr. Redmond. The police had nothing else. That's why this case remains unsolved. Nobody had a real motive. That's why I think everything that's happened was random. And if Larry Ash did it, nobody could catch him in a lie or force him to confess to any part of this."

"Nobody yet," Charlie said.

Emily didn't respond. She took another sip of lemonade and simply stared off toward the gardens.

CHAPTER 14

Later that afternoon, Charlie drove to Springbrook Lane, studying Carla's property in daylight en route to Carla's address, this time, as an invited guest. It wasn't twilight this time around, so Charlie was able to get a better look at her home. As he waited for her at the door, he was able to see how truly quaint her property was, and that it was surrounded by a well-manicured lawn and flower garden. Today, he was experiencing it not as an interloper, but as a legit associate.

"Charlie, thanks for stopping by," she said, appearing almost immediately.

Carla looked even more attractive today, in her domestic element, in jeans and a torn T-shirt. He was glad she'd accepted his invitation to get together.

"Can I get you something to drink, a beer?" she asked, as she directed him in.

"Sure."

Charlie had that good feeling when someone invites you into their house. A giddy feeling, almost, where the chemistry is better, a little warmer than when you see that person in a neutral place. One person reaches out to the other and accepts. Charlie was glad to be there. There was a spark that he could detect from her that confirmed his assumptions, not a spark in a romantic sense, but one that says, we could be friends, it's great to see you, let's pull up a seat and talk.

Once inside, Charlie updated Carla on things, superficial stuff without specific details. They discussed Larry Ash and her mother, Emily Willems. The progress report was little on actual juice but solid on the progress part. For Carla's purposes at this time, Charlie thought, this would suffice.

Yeah, that's why he was at her place. Not because he longed for her. Not because she reminded him of some of the better qualities of his ex. She was sexy and deep. She invited him, after all. Well, he'd called with the first move and said let's get together. But, really, who's keeping track?

Charlie, sat back in his reclining chair in the small living room. Took a swig of beer and looked around her place. This time, he could take things in, comfortably. He wasn't breaking in, trying to make things out under the cloak of dusk, guided by the fact that she might burst through the front door any second and say, "What the fuck are you doing in my house?"

He scanned her bookshelf, able to appreciate her collection. There were some popular literary titles she owned, authors whose books juxtaposed each other on the limited space she devoted to them including Toni Morrison, Stephen King, and James A. Michener.

Thank God there was no L. Ron Hubbard.

"You've got some good books, here," Charlie said. "*Centennial*. I actually read the whole thing."

"Me too," Carla said. "I just love the way Michener takes the concept of local color to entirely new levels."

Charlie forced himself to sound pedantic and exact. "Absolutely. Local color on steroids. I love his descriptions of the hunt for buffalo and the near extinction of the species in the process. The way he wrote about it, almost surgical in its painstaking evolution."

"Believe it or not," she said, "its tone is almost historical enough to be considered by devotees as a narrative nonfiction style. I mean, you could actually sense Michener was reporting on the development of the Wild West as a journalist. I believe it's also referred to as creative non-fiction."

Charlie nodded as if he were conversing with Michener himself, adding a furrowed eyebrow for effect. He rose to meet Carla at the bookshelf, and they stood there silently with their beers. Charlie wondered what she was thinking.

"Did you always want to be an author?"

"Actually, yeah. I haven't been at it for too long. But, yes. I like to write. Did I tell you that? I can't remember. I am writing."

"You did. How's it coming?"

"Slowly. But I'm forging ahead."

I know. I've read some of it. It rocks.

"Your divorce. That's what it's about, right?"

"Yes. Well, it could be about any divorce, I think."

"You can consult with me, if you'd like."

Carla and Charlie laughed. They had another drink and discussed her writing and some of the other titles in the bookshelf. She asked Charlie about being a detective, and he told her some of his tall tales from the job.

Then he said, "So, what's Tom like?"

Carla jerked her neck from the bookshelf to Charlie. "How'd you know about Tom?"

"'Cause he's right here," Charlie said, pointing at the calico, who'd jumped up on the table next to Charlie. "His name tag. Tom."

Whoa. Close call.

Tom had entered quietly, deftly pranced across the floor, jumped up on the table next to Charlie, and sat. He was purring, looking directly at Carla.

"Thomas is wonderful. Does whatever the hell he wants."

"Thomas? Is there another . . ." Charlie caught himself.

"That was his name when I acquired him, well, sorta. Dave, my ex, and I bought him as a kitten from this old couple who've since moved to Kittery. We were leaving their place, when their grandson said we should name him Thomas. So, it stuck. Actually, I just call him Tom. Number one . . . it's easier. Number two . . . it's a cat, right?"

Another close call.

Tom looked at Charlie with huge feline eyes. One of those eyes, just one of them, slowly closed and opened, as if the calico were winking at him, saying, *I know you've been here before.* Tom sprang from the table and slinked out to the backyard, through the sliding glass door, just as Charlie had.

***

Charlie left Carla's place happy, looking forward to updating her in the future, even if he didn't have much to tell her. He thought about their conversations, particularly about the divorce part. He thought about what he had read that night and how much he liked it. He wanted to read more. Perhaps he *needed* to read more. Charlie knew the pain of divorce, how it saddened him to think about Rebecca, even briefly. He thought it was really ballsy for Carla to convey her memories from her divorce in such a public way. He thought about being with his ex, Rebecca, and how he would never be back with her, even though a part of him still loved her and would always love her.

Driving southeast on Market Street along the Piscataqua on his way home, Charlie couldn't help but think of when he and his ex, Rebecca, had met, and the issues that led to their eventual split. She'd been so right for him. But as time went on, he'd seemed to shut down for some reason. She was there for him, at first, but became distant, and sex and intimacy fell by the wayside. She tried to salvage the relationship on her end, suggesting that they should film homemade porn. Charlie recalled that painful episode. He was so numb at the time he didn't put up much resistance and just went through with it. He couldn't remember what was worse: the humiliation of doing such a stupid thing in the name of "therapy," or his ambivalence over the whole matter. Emotional paralysis, he thought.

Rebecca had lashed out at him after the porn episode, saying that if porn wasn't the answer, then she would have to look elsewhere for the intimacy and sex she craved. Naturally Charlie's sex drive had plummeted. Even Viagra couldn't pull him out of the physiological morass he'd found himself in. The more he thought about staying in his marriage, the sicker he'd got. She may have craved sex, but Charlie just wanted out.

To this day, almost six years later, Charlie felt he made the right decision. He remembered the day he left Rebecca, like it was yesterday. He was still a detective in Boston. He remembered the relieved look on her face, the feeling of hopefulness in his heart. He knew, from that moment, he was better off alone. For how long, however, he didn't want to guess.

He pulled into his bungalow's short driveway and thought for a moment, before getting out of his Lincoln. All those raw emotions still affected him in ways he would never understand. His connection with Carla was strong enough to bring those feelings to light. No doubt, it would be therapy for her, and probably for Charlie, too.

CHAPTER 15

Charlie rose the next morning at 6:00 a.m. and went for another five-miler, mentally preparing for his interview with Guy Davis, Emily Willems's biological son from her first marriage. Afterward he dug deep in his closet for a knit collared shirt and underused khakis—the Portsmouth Central Country Club probably wouldn't take well to tatty running clothes—and ran over what he knew about Guy. A glass left eye, according to Carla, left over from a childhood accident. Carla said Guy would fly into a rage if Charlie asked about it.

Charlie pulled up to the country club's front gate.

"You can park anywhere you'd like," the attendant told him, with a look that reminded Charlie of exactly where he was. It was the look that said, you won't see any other Lincoln Town Cars, especially the 1985 cruise ship models that sported a couple of Grateful Dead decals on the rear windshield, anywhere in the lot. There was no snobbery in his look, however. It was more a look of, you're good, I'm glad you're actually here. It's good to see a guest who drives what he wants and doesn't give a shit about what other patrons think.

He probably wouldn't care if I parked all the way at the front of the main facility so all of the members could see my pride and joy on wheels. I'm sure the guard has taken plenty of shit from members here...

"Thanks, dude," Charlie said and drove the Lincoln precisely to where he wanted to park it—directly in the front. He got out, straightened his blazer, smoothed out the wrinkles in his khakis, and walked on the asphalt path that led him to the rear of the clubhouse and the restaurant area. This entrance faced an expansive eighteen-hole golf course. Charlie stood there, appreciating the beauty. Lush green fairways, striking man-made brooks and ponds with gorgeous flowers as far as the club's property stretched. He was amazed at how long he'd lived in Portsmouth and never set foot in a facility like this. He had been to other country clubs as a guest of friends while in his college days in Massachusetts, but none were as opulent as this joint. It simply reeked of money. God knew there was enough aristocracy in this city to justify this place.

Charlie knew a little about the Portsmouth Central Country Club, just enough to question Guy Davis. No entertainment types to be found, Carla Willems and Al Jenkins agreed to that, as well. No bling here. This place, Charlie knew, was propped by Old Money, white money, privileged money, WASP money. He began to stroll toward the restaurant, ignoring looks from patrons sitting at parasol-covered tables. They returned their collective gaze, rather, glowered stares.

If looks could kill, man, I'd be already dead, a thousand times over.

The place was populated by mostly uptight Caucasian men with permanent scowls on their faces, matched in bearing by their stodgy suits and uninspired hairstyles. No smiles here. The joint was oddly peaceful and mundane, with no apparent tolerance for even the least exertional of activities. Anything more than the occasional game of cribbage was probably verboten.

As stylish as the club was, there was an understated air about it. There was no flash. Didn't need to be. That was this joint's charm. He strolled into the club's bistro.

He could see there was more of the same elegant monotony. Groups of elderly, white men eating sandwiches, drinking hot tea, and continuing to give Charlie the evil eye. Charlie knew he looked presentable, yes, but rugged-looking hair on his upper lip and his don't-give-a-shit five o'clock shadow were a little too much for the thick octogenarian presence to accept, including one old guy who nearly tripped over an ottoman staring at him on the way to his table.

"Howdy do," Charlie yelled.

"Wha…," the geezer grumbled, As Charlie passed by.

Charlie approached the bistro's main counter. Musing at the chalkboard menu hanging over the counter, he heard his name called.

"Charlie Redmond?"

Charlie looked to his right, to a man wearing a beret and red ascot about three stools over. He assumed this was Guy Davis. "Yes, I'm Charlie Redmond."

The man stood up and held out his hand. "Guy Davis. Let's have a seat."

They placed their orders—sparkling water for Guy, sweet iced tea for Charlie—after sitting at the nearest table.

"Thanks for agreeing to meet me here," Guy said, with a slight nervous energy. "You're probably feeling a little out of place."

Charlie looked at Guy's glass eye. Here he was, sitting no more than a few feet from a man whose left eyeball didn't budge an inch. It just stared straight ahead, not moving, like a doll's eye. Charlie was momentarily mesmerized, thinking, this would be a good interrogation device.

Close your good eye, better yet, wear an eyepatch over the good eye, and just stare at the interviewee with the glass eye. But then, I guess I wouldn't be able to see. . . .

"Charlie? I asked if you were comfortable here," Guy said, attempting to break his trance.

"Oh," Charlie said, "my pleasure. I'm honored to be here . . . in a weird way, I guess."

Guy gave an uncertain smile. "I find it interesting that you're investigating this case more than a year and a half after the murder. I mean, this is a pretty old case."

Man, it's really difficult to determine this guy's angle with that glass eye.

"I'm a private investigator. I investigate cases like this all the time. Old and cold," Charlie laughed.

Guy didn't.

"Carla hired you, right? That's what Mother told me," Guy said.

Mother? Seriously? Are these the only types of words these people use?

Guy continued. "Great. So, how can I help you?"

Wait, scratch the pencil-thin 'stache. This dude needs a handlebar mustache so he can twirl it while looking at me with both his good eye and glass eye, while wearing a monacle over his glass eye to throw me off, as he laughs maniacally and plots the destruction of the free world.

"Well, your mother was gracious enough to talk with me about Lyle."

"You're aware he wasn't my father," Guy said. "He was Mother's second husband."

God, he's just as defensive as his mother. What do these people have to be so damn defensive about? They've got the world by the 'nads. Damn elitists.

"As you may or may not know," Charlie said, "the cops have yet to identify a prime suspect in this case. There is someone they refer to as a person of interest—"

"Larry Ash," Guy interrupted.

"That's right. Larry Ash. But, he's not why I wanted to talk with you," Charlie said. He paused a beat. "Did you like Lyle Willems, Guy?"

"Mother liked him. So, it follows that I liked him. She made him happy."

"Okay, but your mother notwithstanding, did you like Lyle as a person?"

"How could I not like him? Everybody did, everyone at his company, everyone here at the club. I was a little chilly to him at first, because I didn't want him to replace my father. But, over time, he made it easy to warm to him. I mean, we were never best friends, but we did more than just tolerate each other."

"Many people I've talked to said that he would work odd hours often. That he was really anal retentive at work and came home late."

Guy got to the heart of Charlie's innuendo and said, "I don't think he was cheating on Mother. No one would do that to her."

"You sure about that?"

"Yes, and I'm not the only one who shares that feeling. Tom Liedeman said the same thing."

Charlie stared at Guy.

Guy, in an attempt to recover from a pause an investigator would find suspicious, said almost immediately, "Tom Liedeman. One of the detectives who first investigated this case. He interviewed me. He investigated this whole infidelity angle, and they found nothing. By the way, are you planning on speaking with Liedeman and the other detective who worked on case. . . I believe his name is Lewis. Ray Lewis?"

C'mon, you know his name, you one-eyed snake.

"Tom Liedeman. He moved to Portland. Maine, not Oregon."

"Yes, correct. How did you know that?"

"I know a snitch or two in the department," Charlie said.

"So, you've talked personally with the two detectives that worked on the case?"

"No. But, I do know them by name, like you apparently do. Liedeman and the other, Ray Lewis, you're correct."

Guy Davis's right eye, the good eye, shifted a little. The glass eye just stared ahead. The rest of his body trembled slightly.

Guy said, "So, I don't believe you told me if you were planning on talking to the detectives who were investigating this murder."

"Nope. Why would I do that? Their findings are already in the cold case files," Charlie said, matter of factly, even though he knew he probably would, in fact, follow up.

Guy appeared relieved at this answer, so he took a well-deserved gulp of his sparkling water.

Charlie added, "Besides, talking to those two won't magically produce any new information."

But, I probably will talk to at least one of them. You don't need to know that.

"So, it doesn't look like there's much to go on," Guy said. "What do you do now?"

"Well, just like I'm doing with you. I talk to other people."

"I doubt you'll find anything the cops and detectives couldn't. Really, now," Guy said.

"You underestimate me," Charlie countered. He paused before asking, "Are you upset that I'm investigating this case because the emotional wounds haven't quite healed, or is it something else?"

"Look," Guy said, shifting in his seat, "during this investigation, everyone, police included, started asking if Lyle was having affairs, keeping ridiculous hours, and behaving in this weird way by coming home late, practically every night. Nothing could be further from the truth. All this hearsay made our friends, people in this club, think of, and actually consider, these absurd notions. I don't like that kind of attention, and this club doesn't like it. The cops, detectives, and all the others in the force you apparently know all too well, simply don't care about how assumptions like this hurt my mother and me. Even though none of this is true, they all trumpeted this false information so forcefully that people actually started to believe this insanity. It's been both insulting and beneath us to have to deal with this slander. Please understand that my mother and I would like nothing more than to have this murder solved, but not at the expense of Lyle's good name and my mother's sound reputation. I'm sure some miscreant carried out this awful deed for whatever reason. I really don't know. But I'm sure it had absolutely nothing to do with Lyle. And I *surely* know that he wasn't murdered because of his doing wrong by my mother."

Charlie nodded, pausing for a second or two. "I appreciate your answering my questions, Guy. You've been very helpful."

Appreciative of Charlie's deference, Guy Davis, much calmer now, said, "Would you like a sandwich, or something else to eat before you go?"

"Yes. I believe I would." Charlie smiled.

CHAPTER 16

B ack at home, Charlie was about to take Thompson out for a run, when old lady Bainbridge, the scorned sexagenarian dogsitter, lumbered up to his house. Apparently she was on a mission.

"Whoa, what's up?" Charlie asked.

"Hi ya, Thompson," Bainbridge shouted. "I always acknowledge the presence and power of a canine. Especially one with the staying power of one Thompson Redmond."

"Hear that, Thomps? She's paying you a compliment, you old dog," Charlie said, wondering where the hell this conversation would go.

"Hey, Charlie," Bainbridge said. "Sorry about the outburst the other day. I know that you probably had a good reason to cancel out on our arrangement for the dog here."

"Yeah," Charlie said, looking up at her, as Thompson walked in circles around them both, tethered by his expandable leash. "No big deal. Just out for a walk with my good buddy here. Good to run into you."

"Awesome. Say," she said, "have to tell you there was a man here earlier today driving an obsidian-black Chevy Avalanche, probably an oh-five, or six. Sound familiar?"

Obsidian?

"No, not really. Did you talk to him?" Charlie asked, more engaged with the old lady than he'd ever been.

"I did. I had finished working in my sorry excuse for a flower garden when I noticed him just driving around, back and forth, slowing down when he got to your property. Curiosity got the best of me, so I went right up and asked him what he was doing. I guessed he looked lost, and I noticed that his vehicle always slowed up when he cruised in front of your place. I had to go and see what he was up to, so I did. He told me that he was an old chum from your childhood, and that he kept in touch with you on the regular up until a couple of years ago. He asked me if your bungalow was, indeed, your bungalow. I said yes. Then he told me he was going to surprise you, so don't say anything. I said okay. This was, however, mind you, before I thought he may have been totally bullshitting me."

She paused. Bainbridge cleared her throat then raised her voice with the line. "Charlie, I totally apologize for giving this guy that information about you. Oh, I probably effed up, and I should have known better, you know, considering your line of work and such."

"Please, it's okay. You didn't give him any more info than what he couldn't have seen listed in the phone book or online."

"Okay . . . something else," she said. "I came to determine that this . . . this supposed friend of yours from your past wasn't telling me the absolute truth."

"Let's go into my place," said Charlie. He quickly unspooled Thompson from his legs and walked Bainbridge back to the bungalow. Inside, Charlie made a beeline for the fridge and grabbed a couple of Bud

Lights. They both sat down at the kitchen table. He looked across the table at Bainbridge's frizzled, unkempt hair, and confused expression.

Bainbridge said, after a couple of swigs of beer, "Ahh, good shit. Truly lip-smackin'."

"Indeed," Charlie smiled.

"So," said Bainbridge, "I asked him a couple of questions about where you grew up in Boston and about your ex, Rebecca. Course, I didn't use her name. Made believe I forgot it, trying to test him with it, you know?" she said, clearly growing more excited.

Bainbridge continued. "Kept waiting. Watching him squirm. Making up excuses as to why he couldn't remember her name, in spite of the fact he said he kept in touch with you until recently. He had no effing idea what he was trying to tell me. Effing asshole."

"Cool. That was smart."

"What do you think's going on with this guy?"

"Well, I think I know. This guy I talked to recently is trying to get the 411 on me." Charlie decided not to mention Larry Ash's name.

Bainbridge nodded.

Larry Ash wants to know what I know, or what I want to know from him.

"Yessir," Bainbridge said. "Once he indicated to me through his body language he didn't know what the eff he was talking about, the conversation became suddenly one-sided. He rolled up his truck window and drove off. I will say this. He had a pretty sweet truck. Kinda chromed out."

"What did he look like?"

"Oh boy, I can tell you what he looked liked, yes-siree," Bainbridge said. "About five-foot-nine or so. Thin, balding, dark hair, youngish looking. Really bad skin, though. Probably was a pizza face in high school."

Charlie nodded, barely concealing a smile, thinking of Ash's probable accomplice. "Please don't freak out about that guy. This whole thing could end up helping me, in the end."

Charlie held up his can of beer for a toast with Bainbridge's.

"Mazel tov," she said.

***

Bainbridge gone, Charlie nuked half of a rotisserie chicken in the microwave and prepared some frozen vegetables to complement it. He thought about everything from the case placed into his lap so far. He wanted to mindfuck Larry Ash some, but he still had a little to do to pull it off. He needed to get Larry more uncertain about what was going on, then surprise him. The guy he probably sent to look into Charlie's past? No doubt, Larry had sent some inexperienced private goon in his tricked-out Avalanche trying to appear all official looking.

I'll use this idiot to get Larry more flustered. Then maybe he'll squawk on Lyle Willems.

But now, there were more pressing issues on his plate: Guy Davis and Emily Willems. Charlie understood their feelings on the whole matter. What was more confusing was why they were both hell-bent on reinforcing Lyle Willems's cast-iron fidelity. Why did they both care about this issue so damn much? And why did Guy Davis make such a production of telling Charlie that Detective Liedeman—the same detective who was sent packing to another municipality, with no discipline—had determined that there was no affair, or affairs? There was something contrived about it all.

It seemed like a slip-up on Guy's part. Charlie recalled how just after he said it, he paused and gave him a weird, quizzical look. Maybe Guy said it before he realized he wanted to broadcast to the world who would corroborate his story, just in case.

Maybe Tom Liedeman knew something.

Guy Davis sure as shit didn't want Charlie talking to Liedeman, that part was crystal clear. Guy straight up asked him if he was going right to the police. Charlie could note the worry in Guy's eyes, well even in his stupid glass eye.

Charlie knew that if he just dialed him up, Liedeman would either avoid him or refer him to the police report. So, Charlie did the next best thing: he booked a rental car to Portland, Maine. He thought of Carla. He didn't want to worry her. He'd tell her after he got back that nothing more than a hunch kicked his ass enough to send him on what he hoped wasn't a wild goose chase.

He was going to talk to Liedeman in person. Had to be done this way. This was the cop who had moved. Who had guaranteed, in person, presumably, to Guy Davis that there was no infidelity on the part of Lyle Willems. Who was sent packing to another municipality from his most recent position on the force, without a hint of discipline, but with his pension and benefits intact. Who was nowhere near Portsmouth once the case was declared cold.

Charlie finished the half-cold bird and the mushy vegetables, placed the dishes in the dishwasher, and thought of Carla again. She was the one responsible for the professional state he was in today because she handed all of this to him.

It's all good. I agreed to take this case for Carla, warts and all.

Carla Willems, that dour look, abutted by that sexy, laconic insecurity. All wrapped up in her slightly delicate frame. Those eyes, that strawberry-blond hair.

Man, I wonder what she's doing this very second at her place. Working on her book? Petting her cat? Reading more creative nonfiction?

Any of those scenarios suited his obliging imagination. Charlie stood at the sink, letting hot water run on his hand, until, of course, it got hot enough to knock him out of his reverie.

CHAPTER 17

Charlie got up the next morning and called the Portland PD, asking for Tom Liedeman, knowing it was futile. When Charlie got transferred back to the receptionist, he casually asked, "Um, so's Tom around? Vacation, or anything?"

The receptionist returned, in a tone completely devoid of any investment whatsoever in her job, "Oh, sure he's around," she said. "Just got back from a two-week vacation about six weeks ago, so I think he'll be here, you know, before his next vacation."

Charlie rolled his eyes. "Thanks for your help."

After dropping off Thompson at old lady Bainbridge's, he jumped into his Lincoln and headed toward the nearest Hertz. On his way there, he noticed a familiar vehicle trailing him, about a car length and a half behind—the black Chevy Avalanche. Awesome, Bainbridge was right. That truck was a virtual traveling ball of silver, Charlie thought. He had to squint, the damn thing was so brilliant.

Charlie decided to park his car in a lot off busy Market Street, a few blocks from the car rental, so the guy in the Avalanche would note exactly where Charlie's car was—and could resume trailing Charlie on his return from Portland. Charlie didn't expect to be followed on foot.

Closing in on Portland an hour and a half later, north on I-95, Charlie managed to tease out from the glove compartment a picture of Tom Liedeman that Steve Richards had given him. Thick, round face, curly salt-and-pepper hair, thick black mustache, looked around Charlie's age, mid-fiftyish. Charlie studied the picture as best he could while avoiding running off the road.

He checked in at the Holiday Inn in the heart of downtown Portland, overlooking a picturesque gulf draining into the Atlantic. Very scenic, Charlie thought. He chose this rather pricey hotel because of its proximity to the city's downtown precinct. He was charmed by his room, one of those suite types, with the couch, bookshelf, armoire, coffee table, the whole nine. A little much, but the room was clean, quiet, and, most important, close to his quarry.

It was almost eight in the evening. Charlie decided to just relax tonight, perhaps watch some TV, reconsidering where the case was in his mind at this point. Then tomorrow he'd head to the station to arrange an hour or so of face time with Tom Liedeman. He clicked on CNN and opened his complementary edition of the *Portland Press Herald*. Later he ordered room service that consisted of a salad and a light beer. He enjoyed the calm.

***

Charlie awoke the next morning, bright eyed and ready to seize the day. He promptly went downtown to the headquarters of the Portland PD. He walked into the building and easily found Tom Liedeman's name on the computerized wall listing in the lobby. Charlie got on the first opened elevator and pressed "five," without so much as a glance from the guards.

The doors opened and Charlie approached the receptionist—he wasn't sure if it was the same one he'd spoken with over the phone. Charlie introduced himself. "I don't have an appointment, but I'm a friend of Tom Liedeman's and would like to say hello."

"Let me call him and see if he's back there."

Charlie sat down in the adjacent waiting area. A couple of minutes later, he heard a male voice to his right ask, "Can I help you?"

Charlie looked up and rose, facing Tom Liedeman in a jet-black suit. Charlie had a vague idea of how he was going to handle this interview, but he was unsure if Liedeman would play along. He could only hope.

"Tom, my name is Charlie Redmond. I'm a retired investigator. "

Liedeman, in the expected cop role, maintained his steely look. Stone-faced. Not upset. Not saying anything. He was waiting for Charlie to continue. So, Charlie did.

"I'm investigating a case you worked on, the murder of a prominent medical device exec, Lyle Willems."

"Are you here from Manhattan?" Liedeman asked.

Seasoned cop reply slash question, direct, but carrying some implications. Charlie sensed some surprise in Liedeman's answer. It affected his cop stare because, in that brief split second of surprise on Liedeman's part, he showed some worry, a modicum of vulnerability.

Charlie continued, "Yes, I'm here from Manhattan, by way of Portsmouth. I'm a friend of one of your old coworkers from the force." He stopped short of saying Steve Richards's name.

He seemed engaged and almost interrupted Charlie's tease. "Who's that?" asked Liedeman.

"Steve Richards."

"Oh, great cop," Liedeman said, his guard seeming to drop ever so slightly.

Charlie knew what he had to say next would calm Liedeman down further, that is, if he bought it. "Okay, listen," Charlie said. "This is a challenging case . . . as I'm sure you'll recall. There's just no . . . oh, what's the word I'm looking for . . . *evidence*."

Liedeman smiled, guard down further, but still indomitable.

Charlie plowed on. "I'm here because I heard you were good. I wanted to tease your brain a little, see what you think. I'm working with a lot of presumptions, and I need a sounding board of sorts. You've worked the case, so you have value."

"You came all the way here to ask me if you were making progress in this case?"

"There's a steak dinner in it for you. The Long Horn."

Liedeman seemed to consider the offer. "Going on a couple of years, but I remember the case well. To call it a challenge would be an understatement. If you want me to share some wisdom with you, well, I suppose I can help a fellow investigator, retired or otherwise."

***

Jackpot. How else but to grease the wheels of interrogation with a huge, heaping dose of praise. No one ever gets sick of hearing virtue, especially in this line of work.

Liedeman's guard was no more, and dinner was calling. Of course, Charlie would freely share his ideas. The Long Horn was apparently one of the better-quality steak joints in Portland—stylish, but not pretentious; busy, but not boisterous. Just right for Charlie's purposes. Nothing like a nice steak restaurant with a slammin' wet bar to get a cop talking. Get a cop with a couple of beers or mixed drinks over a nice slab of meat and potatoes, and it was like administering truth serum.

After exchanging a bit of small talk, the men got down to business. At first, Charlie thought they would engage in small talk—life in Portland, in NYC, local sports, politics, whatever. He realized quickly, however, that Tom Liedeman was a talker, and thankfully, one of those guys who liked to hear himself speak. The beers didn't hurt, though.

"Portland is a nice little city, lots to see and do. Can't beat the local culture here. Great place to retire, even. But I have to say, I'm a little lonely, even though I'm not more than seventy-five miles from my last job."

Charlie nodded.

"I took this job because I had an acquaintance up here, the captain, actually. He was getting ready to leave the force. He didn't let anyone know of his immediate plans, but I knew. So, anyway, here I am. Yeah, kinda tough being somewhere new, trying to learn the local flavor on your own. I don't have a significant other," Liedeman sighed.

Tell it to Oprah, or better yet, Dr. Phil.

Charlie listened politely.

The steaks came. Tom Liedeman was ravenous, digging in immediately, forgetting for a moment his social situation in Maine. Now, he was busy eating, as opposed to talking. Liedeman started to speak again, this time saying something Charlie was interested in. "So, what's the latest on the Lyle Willems case?" he asked. "Not cold anymore, I guess. Who hired you?"

"Family member," Charlie said. "Daughter."

"The college prof," Liedeman recalled, taking huge bites of his New York strip. "Smart, kinda hot, as I recall. So, what's up, why do you want my ear?"

"Well, I'm working a few angles," Charlie said.

"Hold on. Let's see. The ad guy and the possibility that Willems was unfaithful?" Liedeman asked, mastication frequency slowing some.

"Right, and something else, the thing I wanted to bounce off of you." Charlie looked right at Liedeman and saw Liedeman register his stare.

"What?" Liedeman said.

"I've been thinking about you, your level of involvement in everything.

Liedeman was listening carefully. Mastication ceased.

"You had an offer here in Portland that you took after this whole Lyle Willems thing went cold. You knew you were leaving."

"Yeah," Liedeman said. "I did."

"Well, I spoke with Guy Davis the other day, and he mentioned you, well, in a way that I found a little unusual."

"So he mentioned me. Big fucking deal. I worked on the case. Why wouldn't he mention me?" said Liedeman, a little more defensive.

"Guy Davis and his mother are desperate to prove to anyone who'll listen that Lyle Willems didn't have extramarital affairs, that Willems wouldn't do that to Emily, embarrass her in that way. When Guy brought your name into the equation, it was almost as if he had a relationship with you, like he knew you as more than a cop. He wasn't happy I might talk to you. So, I got to thinking. Maybe you and Guy had some sort of agreement. Both of you agreed that no matter what you knew, you were going to say whatever Guy wanted you to say."

Liedeman carefully placed his steak knife and fork on the table, measuring his words. "Redmond, this case is a bear. There's absolutely nothing to go on. I feel your struggle to gain in this investigation, but you're trying to create something out of nothing here. That guy mentioned me, all right, so what? Just go back and read the reports Richards furnished you. It's got everything I documented on the case."

Charlie pressed on. "Sure, everything you *wrote* is in the report, but is it everything you *know*? Liedeman, you know as well as I do that detectives don't make much bank. Hell, everyone knows that. Your situation, it's so obvious, from the moment I started talking to you. Let's just say that you had information that Guy Davis had for you and he paid you to keep it under wraps. You were leaving the force in Portsmouth anyway. Who'd be the wiser? You just took a better-paying job in a nice little city, not too far away, but far enough. A lot of cops in your situation would do the same thing."

Liedeman dropped his head down, remaining silent. He finished his beer. Charlie motioned for the waiter, who looked all of twelve years old. He was well on his way to getting Liedeman to spill the beans.

"Let's do a shot or something," Charlie said. "You game?"

Liedeman nodded.

Charlie motioned to the waiter. "Two shots, Scooby Snacks, okay?" he said when the waiter finally came over. He glanced at Liedeman. "You like coconut rum?"

Liedeman nodded his head in agreement. The twelve-year-old waiter was on his mission. They waited for the booze. No one saying anything, Liedeman not as ravenous now, was slowly eating what was left of his steak. Now on to the gristle, chewing away at a tasteless, textureless morsel, desperately trying to avoid Charlie's pointed theories that were hitting home. Liedeman had his head hanging the entire time Charlie sat still, watching him.

He looks like an animal, a wounded one.

The shots arrived at the table. Liedeman stopped chewing his cud, and, synchronous with Charlie, threw back the potent creamy liqueur mix. Liedeman still had yet to maintain eye contact.

Charlie looked at the other detective. "I will not sell you out, Liedeman. Whatever you have to tell me will not come back to haunt you. Please believe me. But if I don't leave this establishment with something solid, something about the Lyle Willems case I don't already know, I will contact his daughter, inform her I'm dropping the investigation, and will investigate you, instead."

"Is that a threat, Redmond? Are you threatening a fellow cop?"

"Yes."

Liedeman's eyes shifted back and forth. "Goddammit, I don't know jack shit. Look, I already told you. You come all this way, and I don't know anything else."

"That's fucking bullshit, Liedeman, and you know it," Charlie said. The shots arrived, and both men doused them.

"You better pay the bill, Redmond."

"Liedeman, for the last time. Tell me what you know, that's all I ask. You can go back to your nice little idyll here in Portland. But if you don't tell me, I will investigate you, even if it means tearing out Guy Davis's glass eye and shoving it down his pretentious throat."

Liedeman laughed, pleasantly caught off guard. It was evident to Charlie that he'd forgotten about Guy Davis's weird ocular prosthetic. He regained eye contact with Charlie.

"Tell me what you know, Liedeman, whatever it is," Charlie persisted. "I just want something, information I need to take this investigation to the next level. Let's just cut the bullshit. You and I both know the information you have is probably why you're up here in Maine, okay? I promise I will not fuck with you. As long as you tell me."

Liedeman fell back in his chair, looking more wounded, but not fatally so. He let out a long, deep sigh. "Well, Detective, you got me. I will tell you what you want to know. What you need to know."

Charlie just stared at Liedeman., who got the message loud and clear to continue. Liedeman said, "I took a payoff from Guy Davis to keep some information out of the final report."

Charlie showed no relief or satisfaction that he'd been right about Liedeman all along. He just continued to stare.

"The only reason I took the cash was because I discovered that the info I had was tangential. It didn't have anything to do with the murder of Lyle Willems."

"So, why did you leave it out?"

"Guy Davis approached me with information. Said it was from Lyle Willems's past. This was information I didn't find on my own. He gave it to me. Said he would give it to me if I'd talk to him first about what info I had already investigated. So, I investigated his info, the info he told me about, and I decided it had nothing to do with the murder. But he wanted to make sure that the info didn't make its way into the official file or become available to the public in any way. I told him that I couldn't do that."

Charlie listened.

Liedeman looked down at his empty shot glass. "That's when he offered me the money."

Charlie's gaze remained fixed on Liedeman.

"I'm a good cop, Redmond. But we don't make shit."

"What did you find out?" Charlie asked.

"That Lyle Willems had an affair."

Charlie nodded.

"We thought that this information was crucial to ultimately solving the case in some way, but we couldn't find anything," Liedeman said. "Then Guy told me about this woman. Said to me that a year or so prior to his murder, Willems's wife, Emily, confronted him about his late nights and not coming home and whatnot. She got pissed. Willems denied everything. But she eventually hired a PI to investigate him. Well, turns out, he was being unfaithful on the side. Emily confronts him with this information, and he stops.

"Guy told me the woman's name and asked me to investigate her possible involvement in the murder. Guy really wanted to keep any mention of the affair under wraps, but he wanted to know if she had anything to do with the murder itself. I hunted her down. Had no problems questioning her. She was nice and all, cooperative. She worked in management . . . in the hospitality industry. You getting all this?"

Charlie nodded and ordered two more beers, both of them for Liedeman.

"So I sat down with her," Liedeman said. "Said she hadn't seen Lyle Willems in over a year's time, basically since Emily ended the affair. She went back to her corporate-type job, and that was that. Lyle was only in the affair for, according to Guy, certain needs his wife wasn't providing. He never promised this woman that he was leaving his wife for her, or any shit like that. No quid pro quos. He just boned her a few times, she said. My investigation of her was essentially a dead end. She found out about Lyle's murder the way everyone else did. After Lyle's wife squelched things, that was it. No more phone calls, e-mails, nothing. There was no connection between them once the affair ended. So, I was satisfied with that. If Lyle Willems's infidelities led him to his murder, then this woman had nothing to do with it. He was killed by someone else, someone we didn't . . . someone yet to be found."

"Does Emily know that Guy told you about the affair?"

"Yep," Liedeman said, sipping a newly ordered beer.

"What's the woman's name?"

Liedeman said, after a profound burp, "I knew you'd get around to asking me that."

"Like I said, I'm not going to fuck with you on this, Liedeman. I already know enough to get you into some serious shit."

Liedeman said with resignation, "You're just going to talk to her about this? You're not going to Guy or anyone else?"

"Scout's honor. You have my word."

"Her name's Brenda Turner," Liedeman said, while he pulled out a card with her contact information on one side. "Damn if I'll admit it, but I figured we'd get to this point."

"Better get you home, Liedeman," Charlie said. "I'll give you a ride, and you can come pick up your car tomorrow."

***

Alone in his rental car, Charlie thought about this new development. Guy and Emily knew about this one affair, the only one that they thought Lyle Willems had ever had. Liedeman had assured Guy that it wasn't connected to the murder in any way. So, when Guy and Emily were being questioned during the investigation, they both were pissed at the accusations, because, as they saw it, Lyle had only that one tryst. And no one else knew about it. The existence of this one affair was the only reason Guy and Emily were positive that the murder wasn't about an affair.

As Charlie put more pieces together back in his hotel room, it became clearer to him that Lyle wasn't murdered for something of material worth—something of value, or influence—that his assailant needed to obtain. He couldn't put his finger on it, but, as the web of intrigue developed about Lyle's lifestyle, this case seemed to be more about a passion killing. Someone with a motive to kill that went far beyond money. Charlie arrived back at the hotel in downtown Portland. Once in his room, fatigue set in, and he stripped off his clothes, got in bed, and turned off the light. He would leave tomorrow morning.

CHAPTER 18

O n his way back home from Hertz, Charlie wasn't
surprised to see the black truck a couple of car
lengths behind. Charlie decided to take the other vehicle
on a little tour.

Charlie, on I-95, clicked on his right blinker, giving
enough time for the Avalanche's driver to prepare to
exit. The truck looked about four car lengths' back. As
Charlie took the exit, the truck followed suit. They were
now heading southeast on Ocean Boulevard, toward
Highway 1. Next, Charlie took a hard left, as if he
changed his mind, deciding not to head toward Rye
Harbor and the beach. Sure enough, the driver of the
Avalanche changed his mind too. Both were heading
north on Banfield Road, back toward downtown
Portsmouth. About a half mile ahead, Charlie remembered a local bike shop, Murray's, he once frequented
for repairs, and pulled into a lot directly across from
it. A couple of minutes later, the Avalanche drove by
toward the end of the block and idled a few feet south
of the next intersection. The vehicle's rear was now
facing Charlie about a quarter mile ahead of him. He
stared at the vehicle for about five minutes. The driver
remained in the truck. Adjacent to the bike shop was an
unfinished two-story building, with two service trucks
parked in front. Each had a placard on the side that read

"Rockland Medical Supply", the durable medical equipment company associated with Larry Ash.

This must be my lucky day.

Charlie got out of his car and headed across the street to the bike shop. He spent about five minutes in the shop as a fake customer before heading out. The Avalanche was nowhere to be found. He got back into his Lincoln, reached under the driver's seat, and pulled out an old digital camera. He knew it wasn't functional because the battery was dead. That didn't stop him from feigning taking pictures of the service trucks, though. After pretending to be a shutterbug for a few, Charlie got back in his car and drove in the opposite direction, toward his place. No Avalanche. Whoever was trailing him must have been content with his (or her) activities for the day. After heading to old lady Bainbridge's place to pick up the dog, Charlie took Thompson for a short walk. Back at the bungalow, he sat down to check his snail mail, e-mail, and voicemail. Then he decided to head back to Bainbridge's place to thank her again for watching the dog and also for alerting him to suspicious activity.

Charlie knocked a couple of times, but no Bainbridge. *Damn, I really want to thank her for contributing to this case.* He decided he would have to catch her next time.

CHAPTER 19

"You know, this is a really cool place for seafood," Carla said. "It's got a great ambience."

Charlie agreed and smiled about her assessment of The Hook, a relatively spendy restaurant overlooking the Piscataqua River Bridge from the Portsmouth side. "I like to take my clients out from time to time during an investigation," he said. "Good for business."

"I appreciate the gesture, but we could have just spoken over the phone," Carla said. "But I'm glad you did."

Charlie did take clients out, true, but none were like Carla Willems. With her, the business-to-pleasure ratio was definitely less than one.

"So Dad did have an affair."

"He sure did," Charlie said.

"And you're sure about that."

"I have a very good source."

"And who might that be?"

"I can't tell you that. Was a deal I made with the source for giving me the info."

"Sure, I understand," said Carla, smiling. "I'm not paying you to tell me everything. Just the one thing I need to know."

What a cool customer, Charlie thought as he sipped his light beer. *This feels like a date. Wonder if she thinks the same?*

"And Larry Ash?" Carla asked.

"Larry Ash," Charlie said, shaking his head in disgust, "is not one of the good guys. I don't know what he's up to. What I'm trying to do with him is screw with his brain. Trying to get him paranoid about things. I'm going to use this plan to find out what he knows."

"How are you going to do that?"

"If I told you now, I'd have to kill you," Charlie said, smiling.

Carla said, in a playful way, "I won't forget."

They placed their orders. Lobster, only for Charlie. Surf and turf for Carla.

"I've been thinking a lot about the book you're writing. You know, what you're doing is brave."

"Thank you. I really appreciate that."

"You're welcome."

"No, I mean, thank you for the compliment," Carla said, "but also for acknowledging the subject matter is a challenging one to deal with emotionally."

"As I've said, I've been there."

Carla continued. "I'm really putting all my heart and soul into this project. I can't say that about a lot of things I've had to struggle with. I guess I'm facing my fears head on. Just getting everything out there in the open. It's so important to me. I don't want to waste my time analyzing myself. Writing about my divorce has given me the strength to deal with this painful period in my life. I'll stop now, pretty sure I'm starting to sound like I'm in an Oprah interview."

Charlie nodded in support. No time for snarky one-liners here. He knew exactly how she felt.

"When I talked to Steve Richards about you, that's what he said," Charlie said.

"He said what?"

"That you did things from your gut. Sure, you thought about things, but you never really had a reason for your pursuits. You just felt like you needed to go forward with them."

"Sometimes, that's the best reason."

After a few moments of silence, Charlie asked, "So, speaking of Richards, did he have any smart-ass snark directed toward me?"

"Oh, maybe a few," Carla laughed.

They ate their food, and it was delectable. Outside in the parking lot, Charlie felt emboldened enough to ask, "Why don't we take a walk on the beach? You know, walk off supper? Not that it was exactly full of carbs, or anything. Tell me more about your book?"

"Sure. Would love to. I don't think I've ever driven to the coastline and just taken a stroll, at night, even. Imagine that," she said.

Charlie led Carla to where he was originally headed earlier in the day when he was being pursued—Rye Harbor State Park and its adjoining beach. She pulled her vehicle, the Escalade, behind Charlie's Lincoln at the first scenic overlook–designated area they encountered. He got out of his car. She got out of hers, and they approached each other. The ocean was on the loud side, waves crashing against large rocks amid all the driftwood.

"This is a nice spot. How'd you know about it?" she said.

"I have my favorites." It was a white lie. Rye Harbor was never one of his most trafficked areas for hiking. But today, it was fresh in his mind.

Make hay while the moon shines.

They took off their shoes and left them by the vehicles. Charlie guided her toward the shore. They walked for a bit, saying nothing, only listening to the trance-like sound of the pounding waves. Then, they stopped.

Carla said, "With divorce, everyone's experience is unique. But in a way, everyone has a shared experience going through the entire process."

"Oh yes," Charlie said.

"No matter the scenario, you learn as much about the other person as you do yourself. Understand what I'm trying to say?"

Yes. But he didn't say it. He just listened.

"Dave and I brought our own personal crap to the relationship," she said. "When you're right there in the trenches, in the middle of it, you start to blame the other person in the relationship. It's as if their problems are the ones directly responsible for the whole damn thing. But then, you don't realize it at first, but if you really take a step back and look at yourself, you see your issues are as much of a problem as his. You may be actually looking at yourself."

"Whoa, that . . . what you just said . . . that should go into your book."

"It's already in there, from day one," Carla laughed.

A few minutes passed, and they became silent once again. Charlie replayed those unmistakably harsh memories of walking away from his ex, slamming the door, and driving away, tire screeches intact, never to return to her.

"You know, it's crazy," Carla said. "But, the weird thing about divorce, and all of the baggage that goes with it, is that you're not immune from the pain that it causes. You endure the pain, the emotion, the self-pity, just get through it as best you can. Then, you yearn for companionship, wanting to try again. Keeping that ember of hope alive for a new and hopefully better relationship."

"Again, that should be in your book," Charlie said, keeping pace with Carla's quicker stride.

She said nothing and kept walking, leaving the sight of their vehicles and beach entrance.

"We probably should turn around," she finally said.

"Yeah, I agree."

"I really had a good time tonight. Thanks again for dinner."

"The pleasure was all mine."

Under the cloudless sky, Charlie could see that the light of the moon made her skin a creamy, soft sight to behold. Carla was literally glowing. *A beautiful glow.* That vulnerability he saw earlier was now gone. He saw something new and exciting about her on this beach tonight. He couldn't put his finger on it, but it made him tingle inside.

They reached their cars and crouched to put on their shoes. From the other side of the beach came a human voice. "Hey, asshole!"

Charlie and Carla turned around to see two guys who appeared to be in their early to mid-twenties. One

Latino male, and one African American male. Charlie thought they resembled gangsta wannabes. Although it was early evening, from the bright moonlight, Charlie was able to make out tattoos of various shapes and sizes on their faces and denim-clad frames. He was able to smell the acrid scent of alcohol once the two were close enough to them.

Charlie said, "Can I help you two gentlemen?"

The two young bangers laughed.

The Latino guy said in a sarcastic tone, "Can you help us? *Can you help us?* Motherfucka, what the fuck the two of you doin' up here on this beach?"

Funny, the Latino guy is trying to sound like the African American guy, who had yet to say a fucking thing.

Carla moved behind Charlie when she heard the profanity.

"We just came out here for a walk," Charlie said. Even though he knew it was dumb to utter what he was about to say, he had a plan. "Look, we don't want any trouble. So why don't you leave us be?" He could feel his heart pounding harder and faster by the second.

The Latino guy continued. "Yo, we here for a walk too. Because we also want your muthafuckin' shit. Yo, your wallet and purse, yo. Hand that shit ova, asshole."

The African American guy stood next to the talker, arms crossed and head nodding

"Well, I hate to break your heart," Charlie said, "but that's just not gonna happen. Sorry." He tried hard to suppress his heart rate and rapid breathing.

The Latino spokesman looked up and laughed an overconfident, condescending laugh.

"Well, Mista Cracka, it looks like I gotta rip yours out, yo. Had enough of your dissin' us, muthafucka," the Latino said, pulling a knife from his baggy cargo denims. Charlie saw that the knife was a short, stubby one with a sharp blade that the Latino guy had to unfold. This was good, he thought, because the weapon appeared to be a tactical knife, not an actual fighting knife, not really suited for close-range individual combat. Charlie felt relieved at this discovery. It gave him more resolve for their escape.

The Latino guy grew more arrogant. Charlie stood mere feet away, with Carla behind him and to his left. His silent African American partner unfolded his arms. Latino guy unfolded the knife and held it up, attempting to make some sort of ominous statement by twisting it in the shine of the moonlight.

Another poseur, though he's got nothing on Larry Ash.

Charlie began to walk toward the two gangbangers.

"Charlie, don't," Carla muttered.

"Hey, yo, hold up. Betta back the fuck up, yo, if you don't wanna knife up yo ass!"

Latino guy could have been talking to a brick wall. Charlie continued to walk toward him, more steadily now. He was about a foot in front of Latino guy when Latino guy, flustered, pulled the knife back. Still moving toward Latino guy, Charlie seized the opening and grabbed Latino guy's right hand, immobilizing the knife and causing it to fall to the ground. He then planted his right fist into Latino guy's face. There was an immediate splatter of blood and a cracking sound. Latino guy was preoccupied, holding both of his hands to his face, crying. His silent partner stood motionless, looking as though he crapped his baggy pants.

Charlie picked up the tactical knife and made a lunging move toward him, saying, "You wanna piece of me, too? Yo?"

Both Latino guy and his buddy looked at Charlie, mortified. They began to run away, but not before Latino guy said to Charlie, "Yo, both you muthafuckas dead, yo. We be comin' back fo' yo' ass."

They ran and disappeared into the night, back to their side of the beach. Charlie, much more relieved now, looked at the knife and turned it so it shone in the moonlight. He tossed it into his Lincoln's front passenger seat. A speechless Carla stood next to him, shaking.

"Well, tonight ended with a bang, no? I actually planned the whole thing," Charlie said, right eye winking.

CHAPTER 20

B renda Turner, Lyle Willems's one-time mistress, happily agreed to talk to Charlie when he told her over the phone that he was investigating the previously cold case. Charlie knew she obviously wasn't privy to the fact that her affair with Lyle Willems had been kept out of the official police report. But she was quite willing to discuss the entire episode with Charlie, willing to be "perfectly frank" about it, she said.

Because of logistical commitments elsewhere, she asked if Charlie could meet her at one of the chain hotels she managed, the Best Western on Portwalk Place in downtown Portsmouth. She told him on the phone that she wasn't a manager, but a *hotelier*, a position that not only demanded years of industry experience, but also an academic degree. Far as Charlie knew, you could hire a couple of unemployed trainables to run the counter, a concierge or two, and maybe a valet, and, presto, you had an operating hotel. So much for expectations.

Brenda couldn't have picked a worse time. It was late afternoon and checkout was occurring with check-in.

Charlie ambled up to the only apparently free staff member at the counter, asking where Brenda's office was. The receptionist gave jumbled directions, making

Charlie seriously question Brenda's leadership and hiring skills.

He found the hallway—the only thing the receptionist actually got right. As he knocked on Brenda's door, he heard, "Come on in."

Charlie entered her office and found it to be immaculate. *Ironic, considering all the chaos she caused Lyle.*

She rose, and after greeting each other they both sat down.

"I was surprised when you called," she said. "It seems like forever since I talked to anyone about Lyle Willems."

Charlie took a glance at the diplomas on her office wall, proving she was in fact a *hotelier*. "On the contrary, you didn't sound surprised at all when I spoke with you on the phone earlier," Charlie said.

"Well, I was. But I talk on the phone so much with my job, I guess I kind of operate like a robot. That's probably why I didn't sound surprised. I probably sounded to you the way I sound to anyone else on the phone, conducting business."

Charlie nodded.

"So, anyhow, I'm happy to talk with you about it, help you out," she said, smiling.

"Great. Thanks," Charlie said.

Charlie studied Brenda. She was attractive, but not compelling, or sexy, just friendly, helpful, a people pleaser with no agenda. She was the antidote to Emily Willems's one-dimensional trophy wife persona that vexed Lyle. Charlie understood why Lyle "could get his needs met" with someone like Brenda. She was a good listener and conveyed empathy to whomever she spoke with, like a caring mother.

"After you called, Tom Liedeman contacted me and said you were coming here to interview me," Brenda said. "I have to tell you, I hadn't talked with Tom since he questioned me initially. But he was . . ." Brenda seemed to be trying hard to search for the right words. "He was nice then, and he was nice when he called. He said that I could trust you and that I could be completely comfortable telling you everything that I told him."

"Yeah, that was nice of Tom."

"Yeah, he's a nice guy."

Changing the subject, Charlie said, "So, how did you and Lyle Willems meet?"

"I met him here at the hotel," she said. "Actually, it was at a fundraiser for a gubernatorial candidate. At the time, I was managing only this hotel. I was pulling double duty and also filling some receptionist duties one night when there was a political event here. Lyle told me that he had to attend functions like this to maintain his fiscal connections, as he put it."

Charlie had to think about how he would ask the next question. Sure, Brenda said that she'd agreed to talk about her relationship with Lyle Willems, but Charlie didn't want to imply she did something amoral . . . or, criminal.

Brenda bailed him out. "Lyle asked me to dinner the following night. I have to confess, I'd looked at his ring finger that night I met him, and I'd seen nothing. I did eventually find out that he was married. It sounds silly and childish, but I was smitten with him. And when he asked me out to dinner, I couldn't refuse. He was witty and engaging, and we also seemed to have similar temperaments—not much of a social life out-side our jobs. That's what drew me to him immediately."

"How many times did the two of you go out?"

"Eight. Well, the eighth being the final time. He called it off on that date."

"What did the both of you do on your dates?"

"Oh, you know, the usual. Dinner, movie, a walk in the park. For some reason Lyle didn't seem too concerned about being seen in public."

Charlie had to ask the next question. "What did you two do intimately?"

"We went to my condo for a couple of the dates. You know, I hadn't talked to him in over a year when I found out he'd been killed."

"And?" Charlie recalled Detective Liedeman's recollection of intercourse.

"And, well . . ." Brenda trailed off, looking down, aware that Charlie knew about the sex. "With benefits, I guess."

"So, you essentially had a very brief affair with him that he ended, and apparently on his terms."

"Right. And I was upset, and so ashamed. Later got over it though. But, yes, I was initially upset because I really liked Lyle. He was so captivating, always telling me about the latest innovations in medical devices, and what it was like to see them get developed. But, God bless him, he was always up front with me, telling me he was married from the get-go. So, from the very beginning I was reluctant to start anything. I really didn't want to keep seeing a married man. So when he called things off, I was relieved."

"When Tom Liedeman initially talked to you about the case, were you nervous?"

"Well, yes and no. Lyle's wife knew about the affair, so there was nothing secret about it. But then I was a little concerned because I didn't know if Lyle's family would hold me responsible, or threaten me in some way. I hadn't talked to him in over a year. Detective Liedeman examined records of my correspondence with Lyle—you know, my e-mails, cell records. He also spoke with my boyfriend who lived with me at the time, and he found out that I hadn't seen Lyle or contacted him in any way in such a long time. The whole thing was very surreal."

"Surreal?"

"Well, weird, I guess. It was weird that I was being questioned about a murder, of all things. Me?"

"Is it weird now?"

"No, not really. I'm more used to it now. Tincture of time, and all that. And I'm really glad I can be of some help to you, Detective. I'm just as confused as anyone about his murder. I can't imagine anyone wanting to kill Lyle Willems."

"Seems a lot of people feel exactly the way you do, Brenda."

Charlie studied her, deciding there was nothing sinister behind her affable countenance. He stood, which seemed to surprise Brenda. Like she didn't expect the interview to end.

"Thank you," he said, holding out his right hand.

Brenda shook his hand. "Oh, uh, you're welcome. Is that it? We're finished?"

"Yes," Charlie said, smiling. "Yes, we are."

CHAPTER 21

D riving home, Charlie thought about Brenda Turner and how he could fuck with Larry Ash. To his surprise, and delight, Charlie spotted a familiar sight in his rearview mirror. The spectacularly scintillating Chevy Avalanche, about three or four car lengths' back, ready for another tour, driven by one investigator investigating another.

Crazy, Charlie thought, that the Avalanche appeared out of the blue, just as he was thinking about the case. This was a perfect time for him to get to the bottom of who the hell this stalker was. Charlie put on the brakes, performed a little deft manipulation on the Lincoln's suspension, and ended up right next to the Avalanche at the next stoplight.

Charlie reached across the passenger side to roll down its window. He motioned to the driver—a balding, dark-haired man with a pockmarked face, just as Bainbridge had described. He prayed the light would stay red awhile longer. Luckily, the Avalanche's windows weren't tinted, and Charlie could make out the driver's features. The driver gave Charlie a "who me?" face and rolled down his driver's side window.

"Hey, could I talk to you for a second?" Charlie yelled.

"What, need directions or something?" the driver asked.

Playing dumb, this guy. Bainbridge got his features down perfectly.

"Nah, I don't need any directions. I just want to talk to you. Find out why you're following me."

"What?" the driver asked, feigning surprise.

"You heard me."

The stoplight turned green, and almost as quickly as it did, the Avalanche sped off. Charlie got behind him and followed closely. The Avalanche turned left onto a tree-lined street in the Atlantic Heights section of the city, deploying standard car-chase moves: last-minute turns, feigned stops, blowing red lights.

Charlie wasn't fazed. He slowed a little, opting for an alternate path to catch his hunter by surprise. He saw the Avalanche turn down another tree-lined side street.

Perfect, now I can make him think that he lost me.

Charlie drove past the turn that the Avalanche made and gunned it.

After about a quarter mile, the truck turned on another side street, this time entering Prescott Park, on the banks of the Piscataqua. Charlie parked about two blocks behind and idled. The truck's driver got out, walked toward a nearby picnic table, and sat down. Never losing sight of Mr. Pockmark, Charlie reached into the glove compartment and unfolded the tactical knife he'd confiscated from the Latino gang banger that night at the beach. Charlie kept his eyes trained on his quarry as he exited his car. He walked briskly for two blocks until he stood about one hundred feet behind the driver, whose back was facing Charlie. The driver pulled out his cell. The ambient noise of children playing covered Charlie's footsteps as he crept closer.

"Hey, it's—"

Charlie slammed his knife down on the picnic table. The driver dropped the phone. "What the—"

Charlie grabbed the phone, checking the caller ID. He ended the call and turned off the phone. He sat down across from the driver.

"How long have you been a PI?" Charlie asked.

No answer.

"I know you've been trailing me, stalking me. You came to my street, my bungalow, talked to my neighbor, followed me down Banfield from the Hertz car lot, and watched me take pictures of the Rockland Medical trucks. Have I left anything out?" Charlie asked, his anger escalating.

A few seconds passed. "Okay. Not long. Few months."

"You work solo, or for a firm?"

"Firm, I, I guess."

"Hmm, a no-nonsense trailing job, so you obviously got the gig."

"Sure."

"Look," Charlie said, seeing the driver tremble. "I'm gonna make this easy for you. Larry Ash—the guy you were calling—is in some serious shit with some bad-asses. A guy named Vincent Contadino, to be specific. Remember that name. Larry Ash knows who the hell I'm talking about. Larry wasn't sure why I stopped by a few days ago, asking him questions about this shit. He was kinda flustered when I talked to him. Didn't know if I was more interested in a guy named Lyle Willems or a durable medical equipment company called Rockland Medical Supply. I know you know about Rockland

Medical because you watched me take pictures of the company trucks.

"I bet you," Charlie continued, "at this very moment, Larry's probably convinced that I'm investigating the medical equipment company. Well, you can tell him he's wrong. Tell him I'm investigating both. And tell him not to contact anyone about this until I contact him. You can bet I'll be getting in touch with him soon."

Charlie glared at Pockmark and said, "You understand everything I just said to you?"

"Sure," Pockmark said, looking at the ground.

"Good."

Charlie got up, pulling his tactical knife from the table. He took a last look at the children playing nearby, hoping they'd missed the encounter.

***

At the bungalow, Charlie didn't have to search hard to find information about Rockland Medical Supply, and Vincent Contadino, online. Their offices were adjacent to some smaller, more nondescript shops in downtown Portsmouth.

The next day at 2:00 sharp, just after pulling up in front of the Rockland Medical building, Charlie spotted Vincent Contadino leaving the building, accompanied by a plus-sized henchman in a tracksuit.

Typical.

But not Vincent "The Shark" Contadino. No sir, he displayed sartorial elegance.

Wonder if he spends every waking moment saying fugheddaboudit *to his hapless hoodlum sidekicks.*

He remained in his Lincoln for almost three hours, staking out the front of the building until Contadino returned with an extra henchman, also in a tracksuit.

Satisfied, Charlie drove home.

Charlie returned to the same spot at 1:50 p.m. the following day. At 2 o'clock, Contadino again left the building with the same two men.

"Excellent," Charlie said out loud. "Good ol' Vince likes to have lunch at the same time every day."

CHAPTER 22

Charlie returned to old lady Bainbridge's later that day and knocked on her door. She was home this time. She opened the front door to her bungalow, and Charlie said, "I need you."

"Oh, my. What? I'm too old fer ya," Bainbridge said, with some shock, as if she was vain enough to consider this more than just a simple housecall.

Charlie did his best to fight back a smile. "I—I'm sorry, Ms. Bainbridge," he began, chagrined, as she opened the front door. "I mean, I need to ask you a favor. I think I'd said I owe you one."

"Oh, okay. Next time, be a little more direct with your exact intentions, capice?" Bainbridge said, not the slightest bit embarrassed by her assumptions. Like it never happened.

Charlie looked past her as he entered her bungalow. He couldn't remember the last time he'd seen the inside of her place. Her sparse living area included only a 1950s-style davenport and a recliner. She had no television set. No computer. The walls were plastered with various still-life photos and paintings. Hardly any available drywall escaped her penchant for such ornaments.

Looks like she raided the local Goodwill's arts and living section.

"Take a seat, anywhere, my friend," she said.

Charlie did as he was told.

"I just wanna tell you that it will be my honor and pleasure to assist the fantastic Charlie Redmond in any endeavor he sees fit to undertake. Ever since you self-lessly intervened, at great peril, I might add, to save my little Blanquito from that awful, mangy junkyard mutt, my death highly probable, HIGHLY PROBABLE, I've always felt like I needed to return the favor to you someday, someway."

Charlie was returning from a mid-afternoon ten-miler one summer day a few years back when he noticed that Bainbridge and her white three-year-old (at the time) Bichon Frise were being tormented by a pissed-off stray that had wandered onto her property. Bainbridge had been coming back from walking her little friend when the rabid dog standing between her and her bun-galow's front door surprised her. No time to think, Charlie found a loose brick from one of Bainbridge's little front yard gardens and immediately foisted it upon the stray's back. The dog yelped and ran off. Bainbridge constantly told Charlie she owed him one. Taking care of Thompson didn't count. She wanted to return the gesture in some special way. Charlie didn't feel as though Bainbridge needed to do such a thing. Even if he had felt that way, he wouldn't have to redeem the favor now, because he knew Bainbridge would want to help him out with a case anyway. This was a major request, how-ever, and so, Charlie figured, a bird in the hand.

Charlie said, "This would be about the case I'm cur-rently working on."

"Fantastic!" she said.

"You've done some acting in your day, right?" Charlie was aware that Bainbridge was a theater major from her days at Nashua Community College. Later, before her bipolar disorder was diagnosed, she did some stints in local TV commercials.

"Well, I want to hire you for a gig. You game?"

"Say no more, Charlie. I'm all in."

***

The following day, Charlie told Bainbridge that he was going to swing back and pick her up just before noon. She didn't ask who she was going to perform for, but Charlie planned on telling her tomorrow that she'd be putting on a show for two men by the name of Larry Ash and Vincent Contadino.

Now all that was left was contacting Brenda Turner.

***

Charlie drove downtown to the Best Western. Before he went inside, he stayed in his car for a few, thinking about what he'd say to Brenda. About why it was *essential* that he had to speak with her once again. He was relieved she'd answered his call and agreed to speak with him again on such short notice.

If there was one most important kernel that Charlie had gleaned during his career as an investigator, it was this: sometimes, your subconscious self crawled out from its safe space and made decisions for you, connecting the dots. Charlie took these "gifts" seriously and treated them with extreme prudence. Your subconscious mind was just as valid as your conscious one. It was relevant, forceful, alive—and right practically all the time.

Sitting in the parking lot of the Best Western, Charlie could feel his subconscious churning away, not necessarily providing any answers, but giving him one clear message: he needed to talk to Brenda Turner once again. He called and told her he was minutes away.

***

The subconscious mind is omnipresent. His often spoke to him during his long runs or hiking treks. It would tell him which roads and paths to take, not the physical ones he would map out prior to his travels, but the metaphysical ones. Like the path his subconscious mind was telling him to take today with the hotelier.

Charlie entered the hotel lobby, this time not needing directions to Brenda's office. She was waiting for him just outside her office door.

"Brenda, I just want to know something," he said.

Brenda's smile faded a little.

"I don't think you had an affair with Lyle Willems."

Brenda just stared. She finally left the doorway and walked back to her desk. Charlie followed.

"It depends on what you mean when you say an 'affair,'" she said, carefully. "I already told you what happened. It really did."

"Brenda, listen, whatever you tell me will not leave these four walls. If you're covering for him, you're not just covering for a dead man, you're also covering for a man who was murdered. There's someone out there who did this. Brenda, to get to the bottom of this, I have to know what really happened with you two. I need to know the truth." Sensing her increasing concern, he said, "I don't suspect you."

The laughter may have left her lips, but Brenda looked fearful. Charlie thought that he would have put her at ease with what he just told her. Instead, she still looked at him, then at the floor. Contorted her face a little.

"I'm feeling a little cooped up in my office," she said. "Can we take a walk? Maybe to the pond?"

"Sure," he said.

***

North Mill Pond was an urban wetland in downtown Portsmouth, surrounded by McMansions and micro-parks—the perfect place for confessions. Charlie parked along the shore bordering Clinton Street, got out, and walked with Brenda along the nearest shoreline path.

"Lyle Willems did strike up a conversation with me that night," she said, curling a strand of light brown hair behind her ear, "and I was flattered by him. We got to know each other better after awhile." She pushed her thin-rimmed glasses to her eyes, smiling at the memory.

Charlie's eager expression forced her to elaborate.

"I guess I got to know him better when he asked me to do something for him."

"Go on."

"Lyle told me his wife thought he was having an affair, even though I knew and he knew he pulled a bunch of all-nighters at the office. At one point, she even had a private investigator tail him. Lyle had to make it stop. So, he had a plan. A plan to fake an affair, get found out, and promise his wife to stop. Then, all the PI stuff would be over with. He tried everything to reassure her that he wasn't sleeping with anyone, but it just wasn't working."

Charlie put the pieces together. "Lyle wanted to make Emily think she found out about him, and this plan would make her believe that an affair existed. Then, he could pretend to end it, and by extension, stop her obsession with it."

"Yes, in a nutshell."

"Did he offer you some compensation, a form of payment for going along with this plan?"

"Twenty grand," Brenda said, walking more slowly. She continued. "I was financially in some dire straits. I knew the money would come in handy. The whole thing seemed innocent enough."

"What happened when you found out that he'd been killed?"

"My best friend from college told me that I should stick to my guns if I was going to be questioned by the cops. You know, tell them that Lyle and I actually had an affair. She thought that saying that he paid me all that money to *say* we had an affair was ludicrous. I mean, who else would know the actual truth? His wife was none the wiser, and she had a private eye tail us, for Chrissakes. No, I really had no other choice than to stick to my story, because if the cops couldn't solve the case, then all I am to the investigation is the woman he paid off to keep quiet about his dalliances."

"Right, you thought that this was a personal matter between you and Lyle. No need to rock the boat because no one else, besides you or Lyle, would know the truth, anyway."

They both quickened their pace along the pond's shore, ignoring the stream of sandpipers flying overhead.

"I had no knowledge of who he told, or whatever. All I can say is that, once I found out he was dead, I decided I'd stick to my original story. I wouldn't make waves. If questioned, I would just admit to the affair. Although people respected Lyle, while shocking on one level, he's human, you know? I'd admit to the affair, because I didn't want any more suspicion drawn to myself. I mean, I'd just say I met him, we got close, did the nasty, and that was that. Plus the twenty thousand he gave me is all gone."

They stopped walking, and Charlie looked at Brenda's honest, friendly face. She only wanted to have a good time that night. She was taken up by Lyle Willems, brought into a situation in which she quickly lost control.

"Lyle Willems never pressured you to take things to the next level?" Charlie asked.

"No, never. I really felt sorry for him, to be quite honest."

"I'm glad you were straight with me, Brenda."

They began walking back to Brenda's car.

"Lyle was a really, really nice guy," Brenda said, a little more emotional. "I could tell that off the bat. I was only trying to help him out." She paused. "How did you know that we didn't have an affair?"

"I didn't. It was . . ." *How do I explain that my sub-conscious did all the work?* "It was just a hunch," he said.

Brenda was expressionless, then grew almost forlorn. "Will I be in trouble?"

"No, Brenda, you won't."

Charlie smiled. Time to put the next phase of his plan into action.

CHAPTER 23

After dropping Brenda off at work, Charlie drove to Bainbridge's, hoping that she'd be ready for her performance. He knocked on her door. She came out, looking as though she'd stepped off a Bollywood production set. He almost didn't recognize her in her flowing black sari, decorated with golden sequins. She also wore two thick silver scarves, one for each shoulder, merging into a loose knot over a silver necklace on her breastbone. They almost covered the thin silver necklace studded with multiple red beads. She wore her graying hair in a loose ponytail that reached mid-back. Although she was able to descend her bungalow's trio of steps, she almost fell forward because of her god-awful black-laced high-heeled shoes.

"Careful there," Charlie said, holding out his hand.

"Why thanks, Charlie," Bainbridge said. "You know, these pumps were the only shoes I could find to match this Indian getup I forgot I had. Took some good ol' fashioned ingenuity, but I was able to fit my sixty somethin' year old ass into 'em."

Charlie was smiling and incredulous. He said, "I guess you still got it."

"Say, got yer camera, or yer phone?"

Charlie pulled out his smartphone and aimed it at Bainbridge.

149

She's getting into this, trying to recapture her youth. How quaint. "Perfect," he said, clicking the shot a couple of times. "You look fantastic, Ms. Finney. Ms. Jane Finney."

"I know," Jane Finney said.

***

After depositing Jane Finney in front of Vincent Contadino's office building, Charlie drove to Instant Fame's parking lot. He got out his smartphone and dialed Darlene.

"Lawrence Ash's office. This is Darlene. How may I help you?"

"Hi, Darlene. Charlie Redmond. How are you?"

"Oh, hey, Charlie. I'm well. I was just thinking about you the other day."

Charlie drifted off a little, blissfully thinking of their come-to-Jesus moment in the Instant Fame parking lot. How hot she looked. How sensitive she was. He had to focus.

"Was wondering if you could send a message Larry's way for me."

"We were supposed to go out for drinks. You never got back to me."

Charlie slapped his forehead. He hoped she didn't hear that. But, she was correct; he never did get back to her.

C'mon, Charlie, get it together. Breathe. Better yet, come up with some sort of itinerary to help you manage this case and your social life. It'd really help you out.

"Oh yeah. You're right. I was supposed to call. I will."

"Okay," she snickered. "Actually, Larry's in his office now. Want me to transfer you in?"

"Nah. Just want you to tell him something for me."

"Sure."

"Let him know that I'm in the parking lot and I want to talk to him for a couple of minutes."

"Okay."

Charlie sat in his Lincoln, looking at large groups of twentysomethings sauntering in and out of the building, giggling and gossiping. Larry walked out of the building a couple of minutes later, looking nervous, ignoring the brown-nosing employees calling his name. Charlie waved his left hand, and Larry rushed over to the Lincoln.

"Afternoon, Larry," Charlie said, through the driver's side window.

"What's the deal?" Larry asked.

"The deal," Charlie said, "is about you. A little more specifically, this is about your relationship with Vincent Contadino. Ever heard of him?"

"Yes, I have. I work with him. He's got a durable medical equipment company." Larry looked to the side. "Look, I'm very busy . . ."

Charlie ignored him. "Did the PI you hired to trail me relay my message?"

Larry stared over the Lincoln's top, then back at Charlie.

"Get in. Now."

Larry walked around to the Lincoln's passenger side.

"Got some smokes in the glove compartment and a lighter, if you'd like. I don't partake, but, if my clients and associates are so inclined, I offer," said Charlie.

Larry looked at Charlie, said nothing, and returned his gaze forward. He seemed to swallow the lump in his throat.

"Okay, this is what's up. Vincent Contadino doesn't have faith in you anymore. Honestly, he just doesn't trust you. How did that happen? Well, he believes you're the type of guy who could turn the tables on him and send him up the proverbial river. Get him into deep, deep trouble. When he believes some jerkoff is trying to screw him, he, well, gets upset. Very upset."

Larry shot back, saying, "Vincent Contadino doesn't think I'm out to screw him. He's in business, and I floated him some funds."

"Hard-headed sonofabitch you are," Charlie said. He started the Lincoln.

"Hey," Larry said, "where are we going?"

Charlie didn't say anything, and instead pulled out onto I-95, headed toward downtown Portsmouth. The following ten minutes were excruciating for Ash, as they pulled into the Rockland Medical Supply offices, just as Contadino stepped out to lunch.

Charlie turned to Larry. "Check it out. I want you to watch this."

He motioned to the building's front entrance. At precisely two o'clock, Contadino exited, with two of his men.

"See that guy to Contadino's right?" Charlie said. "That guy is one of his principals."

"Yeah," Larry Ash said, nodding.

Charlie and Larry Ash continued to watch as Bainbridge—Ms. Jane Finney—walked toward the three men. The four shook hands, and Bainbridge handed Contadino a manila envelope.

Larry didn't know that inside the envelope was a gift voucher for the Seacoast Taj Mahal, one of Portsmouth's better Indian restaurants. Jane worked there, and was reaching out to new, successful business owners in the local community by offering gift certificates for free dinners. Something of a thank you, she explained to Contadino, for simply choosing to do business nearby. Contadino took the envelope and smiled broadly.

"Okay," said Charlie to Larry, "see that? Inside that envelope is information on you."

"On me? What do you mean, on me?"

Charlie shifted the idling Lincoln into drive and turned in the opposite direction, until he found an alleyway.

"Remember that time I first came to your office, and you really couldn't get a handle on what I was fishing for, exactly?" Charlie asked as he pulled up in front of a Dumpster blocking the exit.

"Yeah." Larry nodded nervously.

"Well, it's like this. I work for Vincent Contadino. We were trying to get info on you."

Just then Bainbridge appeared behind the Lincoln and approached Larry Ash's window, a scowl on her face. Charlie watched as beads of sweat appeared on Ash's forehead, and both his hands shook.

"Larry," Charlie said, "you're in some deep shit. This," he said, pointing to Bainbridge, "is Jane, an associate of Contadino's. Like I said earlier, Vincent Contadino thinks you're going to get him into trouble. He thinks that you suspect him of malfeasance."

"Let's get out of the car. C'mon, Larry," Charlie admonished, delighting in the abject fear in Ash's eyes. The two men exited the Lincoln and met between the vehicle's wide grille and the Dumpster.

Bainbridge moved in a little closer to Larry Ash.

"I don't have any clue what Vincent Contadino has on me," Larry said, backing into Charlie. "All I did was invest in his company."

"Vincent Contadino hired me to get shit on you because, as far as he was concerned, you were the type of asshole that might question things," Charlie said. "Like after I came and talked to you that day, you turned around and hired someone to trail me. Why did you do that, Larry?"

Larry's lips opened and closed, as if he actually wanted to say something, but he could only muster a headshake, no.

"I'll answer for you," said Charlie. "You did that because you think that Vincent Contadino has some shenanigans going on, right? Yes, you made an investment in his medical device company, but you didn't make that investment confidently. You were suspicious from the get-go. Once you found out I was taking those pics of Contadino's building, you thought, bingo! Contadino's the real asshole here. Contadino definitely can't deal with that. You couldn't either. You reconsidered your dealings with Contadino. You needed something on him. So you had me tailed."

"No! No! I—I hired the private investigator so I could tell Contadino about *you!*"

"Well, you know what, Sherlock?" Charlie said. "I call bullshit. And so does Contadino. You wouldn't have hired someone to follow me if you didn't think Contadino was on the up-and-up. And, like I said, Contadino can't tolerate that."

Bainbridge opened her costume Narlai bag and pulled out a .38 Glock. Larry Ash didn't know that it wasn't loaded. He'd never know it.

Larry Ash jumped again, landing on Charlie's shoes. Bainbridge moved even closer, but not pointing the weapon at Larry just yet. She finally delivered the first line in the scene: "Tell us what you know about Vincent Contadino."

"Look, I don't know anything," Larry said. "Swear to God. I don't suspect him of anything. Never did. I have never said anything to anyone about the way he conducts his business."

Bainbridge advanced, causing Larry to fall to his knees and put his hands on the ground. He sucked in air, breathing deep.

"Now is the time to be completely honest with us, Mr. Ash," Bainbridge said.

"I swear. I don't know anything. Please, please. Don't hurt me," Larry begged.

Charlie considered his position. He knew that he had Ash at his most vulnerable point in this investigation. Clearly, Larry Ash was convinced that this was a serious situation, and honestly thought he'd be killed. Before Charlie could think any further, Bainbridge asked, "Tell us what you know about the murder of Lyle Willems."

Charlie tensed. The question had absolutely nothing to do with Vincent Contadino—would Larry notice? That he was using Larry Ash's relationship with

Contadino to get intel on Lyle Willems? That Charlie forced the ruse that kept Larry Ash thinking that it could be about Lyle Willems . . . so Larry wouldn't talk to Contadino before Charlie had a chance to carry out this intricate plan? Not a chance, Charlie thought. This poor soul was on the ground, begging for dear life. Charlie decided to roll with it.

Larry's elbows buckled, and he looked at the ground while he spoke. "Nothing. Not anything. He was a business competitor. I had nothing to do with his murder. Oh fuck, I think I'm gonna puke."

Bainbridge gently pushed the Glock against Larry Ash's right ear, so that he would raise his head. "I will ask this only once more," she said, in a monotone voice. "What do you know about the murder of Lyle Willems?"

On all fours, Larry Ash looked up, eyes full of tears. "I promise," he said. "I don't know anything about the murder. I—I don't."

He looked up in Charlie's direction. "Please, tell her I don't know why or how Lyle Willems was killed. Please tell her not to kill me."

Charlie knelt down next to Larry, placing his right hand on his shoulder. "Larry, what do you know about Lyle Willems that I don't know?"

Larry Ash gave Charlie a desperate look. "I used to follow him closely," Larry said.

Charlie motioned Bainbridge to back off. He looked at Larry, moving a little closer. "What do you mean by following him closely?"

"I was obsessed with Lyle, okay?" Larry said. "He was one of those people who had everything—the business, the accounts. I had to find out what made him so fuckin' . . . successful. It got to the point where I was showing up at some of his company meetings, saying I was invited. I was always let in because I told security we'd been in contact, and I was working on potential ad campaigns for products that were going to be out of development soon."

Larry scooted over to the side of the alley, where he rested his aching back against a concrete wall. Charlie sat down in front of him, while Bainbridge remained standing.

"There was a brief period where he wouldn't go anywhere interesting," said Larry. "He'd just go to the office from home, and vice versa. But I didn't care. I'd follow him regardless. I know it was pretty fuckin' sad . . . crazy, even. It got to the point I thought I was the more fucked-up guy for following him everywhere. Then on one occasion, I tailed him when he left his house alone and drove downtown, to a swanky massage parlor located in one of those fancy strip malls on the edge of town. I followed him, but I parked about a block or so away."

"He was getting massages?" Charlie said. "What's so strange about that? Guy worked hard. Probably needed 'em."

"Well, that's what I thought, until I got the courage to go inside, myself. I had tailed him a couple of times to this place, and he always would spend twice as long as someone getting one of their longer massages would receive.

"After three or four visits to this massage parlor, following Lyle, I decided to go on my own. I made sure to go when he usually went. That evening, it happened to be when he actually went to work. When I got there, I was pretty surprised. It was a pretty big place, with multiple rooms, but there was no one there.

"Then this woman comes up to me, asking if I wanted a massage. I thought that maybe she was the manager, or owner, or something. Only thing I can remember about her is that she looked like she had fake tits. She comes up to me and says, 'Can I help you?' I said, 'Well, I think so.' Then she said, 'Do you want a massage?' I said, 'No, I don't.' And she said, 'Well, how can I help you? Are you in the right place?' I just kinda looked at her. She looked at me for a second then asked me for my card. She left me and went to her desk to call my assistant. Apparently Darlene wasn't there, and the owner, whoever she was, didn't leave a message. I guess she was thinking I was the fuzz or something.

"Then she comes back to me and says, 'Okay, the show's a grand.' I thought to myself . . . what's this guy into? A thousand bucks? The hell? So I paid her and went to one of those session rooms to the side. It just got freakier after that. First, a fat-ass woman came in. Musta been over four hundred pounds. She started to take off all of her clothes. Then she started to writhe around and shit, really weird. She wasn't sexy at all . . . that's for sure. All that was missing was a greasy pole, or some shit. Anyway, a few minutes later, a much more attractive and hot babe came in, same height as the fat chick, but a helluva lot hotter. Bodacious body. I could go on. And, she took her clothes off. And then the both of them started to make out. So fuckin' weird, I gotta tell you."

Charlie and Bainbridge stared at each other in amazement at how quickly Larry Ash relaxed as he spun this story. Either he completely forgot how close he thought he was to death, even though he was nowhere near the sickle of the grim reaper, or he lost track of how liberating it was for him to set himself free by coming clean.

Larry Ash continued. "The show took a long time, well over two hours. I actually lost track of time, believe it or not. I stopped tailing Lyle after that. Guess I was a little embarrassed about witnessing something like that."

Larry Ash sat on the side of the alleyway, legs bent at the knees, back resting against the concrete wall, and he looked down at the ground between his legs. He raised his head slightly and flashed a pathetic grin. He said, "I really don't remember why I quit following Lyle Willems that night. But I never told anyone else about this until today, obviously. I mean, you know, what's more fucked up? The Great Lyle Willems going to a live lesbian sex show, or me actually following him to that place and . . . uh . . . liking it, well . . . just a little."

Charlie drove Larry Ash back to Instant Fame. Bainbridge was shotgun. The entire trip back to Larry Ash's place of work was completely silent. Just the sound of Larry's deep, guttural breathing breaking the uneasy ride among the din of ambient street sounds.

Charlie pulled into the parking lot, put the Lincoln into idle, and said to Larry Ash, "Vincent Contadino absolutely does not want to know about any of this. Like it never happened. Understand?"

Larry Ash, happy in his mind to be alive, stared at Charlie and said, "What do Lyle Willems and Vincent Contadino have in common, then?"

Charlie just looked right through Larry, and Larry rolled his eyes.

"All right, you know, I don't care," said Larry. "There's no reason to even think about it."

Charlie gave a quick nod and watched as Larry headed toward the building. Charlie and Bainbridge, formerly of her brief acting stint as Jane Finney, watched him walking back to his ad agency. Bainbridge said, "Was I a help? Didja get all the info you needed on this guy for yer investigation?"

Charlie said, "Sure did. And Larry Ash had nothing to do with Lyle Willems's murder. I no longer suspect him."

Bainbridge got out of the backseat and sat beside Charlie on the passenger side. Charlie smiled at Bainbridge and said, "I gotta tell you, your performance was flawless."

"Why, thank you, good sir."

"Oh, and also, when Contadino goes to the restaurant to redeem his gift certificate, he'll have a good time and a great meal. He'll also be told that the owner, who's long since moved on to bigger and better things and sold the place to someone else, regrets that he couldn't service him because he had to return to New York permanently to take care of his close brother who's dying of terminal cancer."

"A very exemplary thing for him to do."

"You know it."

Charlie motioned to his glove compartment. Bainbridge opened it and spied a couple of smokes and a lighter. "You mind?" she said.

"Got your name all over 'em," Charlie said.

Bainbridge rolled down her window and blew out a couple of puffs. She seemed to enjoy the early evening air while savoring her comeback performance.

"Oh, and Larry Ash?" Charlie said. "Don't worry. He'll never say anything to Vincent Contadino."

"I know," she said, laughing.

CHAPTER 24

After a restful night's sleep, Charlie felt ready to head to the massage parlor. He wondered if he should see the whole Brenda Turner ploy in a new light. Was she paid to keep Lyle Willems's meddling wife from finding out about a silly sex show? Lyle Willems was known for going all out in business, but paying Brenda twenty grand just to pretend to have an affair with him seemed excessive, too. Why would he go to similar lengths to hide the fact that he liked to watch two hot chicks get it on? At the end of the day, it was just two women having lesbian sex. Real-life amateur porn. Why was it so damn important to him that his wife not know what he was doing?

Lyle had the means to do all sorts of covert things, but he could have done them much easier, Charlie thought. He was always on the move, practically nomadic. No one probably would have ever noticed anyway. Why was Lyle Willems so extravagant?

And then there was Emily Willems. Why was she so hell-bent that her husband was having an affair? *We loved to talk about movies and plays and business. We had an intellectual relationship. . . .*

How odd. Hiring a PI to follow your husband was pretty lowbrow. Did Emily get paranoid because of trips downtown for massages, or was it something more sinister? Something even Larry Ash didn't suspect?

Charlie racked his brain. What was Lyle Willems's motive for paying off Brenda Turner to help him pull off that scenario of infidelity? Charlie *thought* he knew Lyle's psyche behind this whole ruse. What was wrong with simply admitting to the dalliance so that his wife could get off his case and let him go about his career with a clean conscience? Lyle and his wife loved each other, in their eyes, and in society's view of their marriage. It may have not been a particularly adoring matrimony at all times, but it was a solid union. Again, why go to such lengths? Why was it so damn important to him that his wife not know what he was doing?

The truth was, Lyle had a talent for exploiting others, for better or worse, to suit his needs. He manipulated his wife's rationale and twisted it in a grandiose manner. One grand, twenty grand—those amounts meant nothing to Lyle Willems. Just another means to an end, Charlie thought. And true to form, it worked.

Charlie liked downtown Portsmouth. Classic late seventeenth century brick architecture juxtaposed with modern restaurants and eclectic twenty-first-century niche shops and boutiques. It was about as big as a city could get in New England without losing that sensibility. Although he loved the character of downtown, Charlie knew it entirely wasn't for him. Not much of a reason for a fiftysomething retired detective to consort with leather-clad, tattoo-loving, body-pierced goth millennials over coffee. It was just nice to take in the city and think, all while plotting his next moves.

Charlie headed north on Hanover Street, then northwest on Market Street until reaching the city's northwest border. There, he found the massage parlor, flanked by a dollar store and hardware store. A red-lettered sign read LOTUS MASSAGE.

Charlie parked the Lincoln in the parking lot directly in front of the massage parlor. He remained pensive for a bit. There didn't seem to be any patrons; nobody went in during the twenty minutes he stayed in his vehicle. Then he got out and walked in.

He stood inside, looking around. The front lobby was a fairly tight affair with narrow hallways running from the desk directly opposite Charlie. It had private rooms for god knows what. Charlie heard one of the rear doors of the hallway on the right open and close. A thin Asian man approached him from the hallway.

"Can I be of help to you, sir?" he asked.

Charlie recalled that Larry Ash's welcoming party was a female. Both men stared at each other for a moment. Charlie thought that the guy looked perilous; despite being slight, the man seemed as if he could take Charlie down in a fraction of a second with some jujitsu move. Maybe it was the weird glint in his eyes.

Charlie feigned a weak smile. He asked, "Oh, I was looking for a restroom. I really gotta go."

"Only for customers here." The man paused. "Are you a customer?"

Charlie looked at him. It got a little warmer in the room.

"I've gotta go something fierce," Charlie said. "Too much diet soda. I tried the store next door, but they said it was out of commission. Please?"

The thin man gave a steely laugh and said, "Sure, guy. Let me show you where it is."

He led Charlie down the other hallway, the one ahead and to the left of where Charlie stood. They passed five doors on the right side of the hallway. The thin man opened a sixth door directly in front of them. Amazingly, there was another narrow hallway that seemed to curl around the rear of the building, lined with still a few more rooms. By the time they arrived at end of the hall, the bathroom was clearly marked and was the last room they encountered. The thin man said, "This is the bathroom."

Charlie mused that this guy could have just given him directions that ended with something like, "It's the very last door directly in front of you that's marked bathroom." *He led me back here personally. Maybe he wanted to make sure I didn't open any other doors. . . .*

Charlie went inside. The thin man didn't appear to want to leave Charlie alone and stood outside the door as Charlie shut it behind him. He actually did have to piss. He could see the shadow of the man's feet under the closed door. After he flushed the toilet, Charlie thought he heard a female voice talking to the thin man. He washed his hands and regretted having to use the air dryer, no paper towels in sight, as it would drown out what he thought he heard.

I'm all for the environment, but man, this was not the best time to be green.

Once the machine automatically stopped, Charlie heard nothing. He opened the door. The thin man was still there.

Looking at the man, Charlie said, "Hey, you're a lifesaver."

"No doubt," the thin man said, expressionless.

The thin man motioned Charlie to walk ahead of him back to the lobby. Charlie nodded at the thin man and began the labyrinthine trek back. He looked straight ahead as he walked, the thin man's clipped steps never more than a couple of steps behind him.

Back in the lobby, the two stared at each other. Charlie wondered how this guy played out in the strange backstory of Lyle Willems's murder. Thinking further, Charlie considered asking him about Larry Ash, or perhaps Lyle Willems himself. He decided against it. This guy looked intense, yet tranquil. Like a powder keg just about to pop. *Now's not the right time to delve into this. And he's certainly not the guy to ask.*

"A thousand thanks," Charlie said.

The thin man looked at him and winked his right eye, catching Charlie by surprise. In that split second, Charlie saw before him a placid man who nonetheless promised evil.

CHAPTER 25

Charlie left the strip mall and drove back toward downtown. Almost as quickly as he left, he reconsidered things. He made a U-turn as safely as he could on Market Street and headed back toward downtown's outskirts, toward the strip mall. This time, he pulled the Lincoln behind the mall, in an adjacent alley. From his vantage, he spied the rear facades of the westernmost stores in the mall—the thrift shop, the hardware store, and the massage parlor. He surveyed his immediate surroundings. Luckily, there was a more covert location where he could hide his car. Toward the western end of the alley, he could see another recess that appeared just wide enough for him to back his boat-on-wheels in and observe straight ahead the action behind the massage parlor. He backed in, turned off the engine, and waited. Twilight turned to dusk.

Employees from the nearby stores headed out to their cars. Charlie saw the rear door of the massage parlor open, and watched as a thin Asian man (the same eerie guy he'd just seen) headed over to his Range Rover. A few minutes later, a blonde woman left from the same rear door, and got into a beige Chevy Tahoe—at least that's what it appeared to be under the dim rear parking lot lights.

Charlie waited until she backed out, then cautiously pulled out of his hiding place. He followed her down Market, toward downtown, then down Hanover and Congress. Finally she turned north onto State, and stopped at a bakery on Marcy Street, near the foot of the Memorial Bridge.

Charlie found a spot about half a block away and turned off the Lincoln. He got out and sat on the Lincoln's hood, his eyes trained on the bakery.

A few minutes later she exited, and Charlie advanced toward the SUV. She fumbled with her keys, but finally found the button to gain entry. By this time, Charlie was directly between the bakery entrance and her vehicle. As she started the ignition, Charlie, unconcerned about his incivility, opened the passenger door, lightning quick, and got in. He squelched her scream by placing his left hand over her mouth. Though he felt uneasy about it, he had to play the heavy.

"Calm down, sweetheart. Portsmouth PD. I'm a cop."

She stared at him, wide-eyed and motionless. Charlie slowly removed his left hand. He could see a can of mace on her keychain, which she held in her right hand.

"Don't you even *think* about spraying that in my direction. Put your keys on the floor. Now."

The woman did as she was told.

Charlie kept his eyes on her as he reached for her keys. He considered her for a second. *She was pretty, but in a skanky adult movie way. Not beautiful, but artificially attractive, like her boobs, like everything about her.*

Charlie said, "I know all about you. I know about your boss. I know what you do. But, you want to know something else? I really don't care."

She never took her eyes off him. She was scared, but she also had a determination about her. *In her line of work, she's probably been in these types of scuffles with undercover cops before.*

"I'm going to show you some pictures," he said. "I want you to tell me if any of the people in the pictures has ever partaken in the entertainment your establishment provides. We've been casing your joint for a while now, and all we want to know is if certain persons of interest are coming in. We aren't interested in your day-to-day operations, just certain people." *If I really was interested in how you did business, you'd be out on your ass, and probably in jail now.*

Charlie reached into his right cargo pocket and pulled out a picture of Larry Ash.

The woman seemed to calm a bit. "Yeah, sure, he came in. Once, maybe twice."

Charlie nodded at her. "All right, now for another." Charlie held up a picture of Lyle Willems. "I want you to tell me the same thing. Has this guy ever been to one of your shows?"

"Nah, I don't think I've ever seen him before."

He wondered if she was lying. Was she involved with Lyle or was she telling Charlie the truth?

"Is it possible that you haven't ever seen him, but someone else has?"

"Yeah, I guess. If he came in once, or something. But most who come are frequent flyers. So I would say, no, I've never seen this guy."

"You sure?"

"You're a cop, right?" she said. "Well, if so, why don't you just get it over with and shut us down? What difference does it make to you who comes in or who doesn't, if you can get rid of us anyway?"

Charlie held up Lyle Willems's picture. "It's like you told me. Your customers return. We want this guy to return."

"Well, I don't think he's ever been in."

"As for me and the guys at the force, now we know."

"Okay, so now that you know, as you put it, will you be shutting us down?"

"Not if you stay quiet."

"About what? Our business, or you jumping in my truck?"

"Both," Charlie said. He opened the door, threw her the keys, and got out.

CHAPTER 26

Charlie sat on his front porch rocker nursing a Bud Light, thinking about the day's events and how they could possibly be intertwined. If there was ever a time his subconscious could give him a hand, it was now. He looked down at his snoring dog and gave him a couple of mercy pettings.

"Who's telling me the truth, Thomps, and who's not?"

Charlie took another gulp. He didn't think Larry Ash was lying. Not after the grilling he and Bainbridge gave him. But what about Lyle Willems? Had he inadvertently gone into the parlor for some innocent reason, like to use the restroom, as Charlie had done? Maybe the blonde woman from the massage parlor was telling the truth and simply missed Lyle coming in the one or two times for a legitimate experience? One thing was for sure: Larry Ash got an eyeful.

But was the blonde woman lying about things to protect her boss, the thin man? Was he her pimp? And why would she lie about Lyle if he'd only been there a couple of times? Further confusing him was the fact that she'd admitted to seeing Larry Ash, who'd only visited once, and not Lyle.

Charlie looked down at Thompson, who stirred.

"Boy, tell me what I should know. Lyle Willems said he had an affair, but really didn't. He went into a massage parlor on the outskirts of town and may have seen a live sex show. Or, maybe he didn't."

Thompson looked up at him, then pushed past the doggy door.

"Well, that does it," Charlie said. It was time to call Steve Richards.

***

Charlie drained the last bit of beer from the can and looked out toward the Piscataqua. He noticed his smartphone buzzing on vibrate. He didn't recognize the number. He answered.

"Charlie Redmond."

"Charlie, it's Darlene," the voice on the line said.

Oh, snap. Darlene. Shit, why do I keep forgetting to call her?

"I thought we were gonna get together," Darlene said. "We made a deal."

"You're right," Charlie said, exasperated. "Where are you now?"

"I'm just leaving work."

"Okay, I'll meet you at Loco Coco's. It's Tex-Mex. Heard of it?"

"Yep, it's in Kittery. Love it. See you there."

The call to Steve Richards would have to wait.

***

Twenty minutes later, Charlie reluctantly left his bungalow. Not because he didn't want to join Darlene Connolly and it's a sight for his eyes, but because he was still no further along in solving this case than he was a few weeks ago. He was frustrated. Perhaps he needed to get out and enjoy himself, whatever that entailed. Maybe inspiration would come to him when he least expected it. Subconsciously, it'll likely involve sex.

When he arrived at the restaurant, he had no problems picking out Darlene. There she was at the wet bar, mixed drink in hand. Stunning as ever, he thought to himself, approaching her. I'm sure all these people watching me are probably thinking, who's the lucky bastard hooking up with this chick at the bar? He actually didn't care what others were saying. All he cared about was her awesome body and how it was beckoning him to her. How it was so well proportioned that it defied logic. It was full in all the right places and leaner in all the right places. He finally made it to her personal space and sat down next to her at the bar. She didn't flinch.

"Darlene. Hi. You're looking fine tonight."

"Thank you, Charlie."

Focus, Charlie, focus. Remember, you're still trying to summon your subconscious.

"So, what I wanna know is, what did you talk to Larry about? When he finally returned to the office, he looked really shaken . . . scared."

"I just asked him a few questions about the case. You know, some things that I forgot to ask him at his office that day."

"Well, I'm thinking you should probably question him more often. When he came back he gave me the rest of the day off. It was pretty sweet."

Charlie chuckled quietly. She smiled at him. Her body smiled at him.

175

"Are you okay?" she asked. "I'm glad to see you, finally. But you look a little stressed."

"I was afraid you'd see that. Pretty obvious, huh?"

They ordered a round of drinks—his first, her second. Charlie took a couple of sips and looked around the bar and the restaurant. He liked bars more on the Maine side of the Piscataqua. They seemed, well, more real. Not as yuppyish or corporate as the stuffier places on the Portsmouth side. Just good old-fashioned, working-class people in for a couple of drinks during happy hour and nothing else. He felt more relaxed.

"Does this have anything to do with the case you're working on?" Darlene asked. "I mean, you don't have to say anything if you don't want to."

Another great thing about this woman, Charlie thought. She was respectful. Never prodding. If she thought that she might be compromising his activities as a detective, then she would back off and accept whatever he could or couldn't share with her. Because of this, he thought he could.

"I'm investigating the death of Lyle Willems."

Darlene paused. "Does Larry . . . ?"

"Don't worry. I don't suspect him of anything," Charlie said. Then he smiled and said, "But, I still think he's an asshole."

Darlene smiled back and said, "I remember when Lyle was killed. I was just starting in the advertising biz. Even though I never met him, it didn't take long for me to become aware of him. He was like a god to so many in the medical device and ad biz. I just can't believe I'm connected to him now. I mean, because I'm sitting here having drinks with the guy investigating his murder. Talk about your six degrees."

Charlie ordered three more rounds of drinks. Darlene switched to Diet Coke. She got up from her barstool and stood behind Charlie. She began to rub his neck, in a massage type of motion. Charlie downed another drink and turned to look at her. He groaned in pleasure and smiled at her. Maybe all he needed was a hookup to relieve his creative impasse.

Standing behind him and rubbing his neck, Darlene said, "How's this for getting that stress out of your body?"

"It feels fucking fantastic," Charlie slurred and turned around to face her.

"Have you ever thought about it?" Darlene chuckled.

"About what?"

"About recreating what you and Rebecca did online."

"My ex? Kinky Bastards? That damn website? Hell no. Forget it . . ." Charlie said, moderately buzzed. "I might be drunk. But I'm not stupid."

"Sorry," she laughed. "I know, I didn't mean anything by it. Just wondering how with it you are."

"With you . . . you mean," Charlie laughed, and then burped.

"I've got a better idea."

"I'm afraid to ask."

"Let me drive you back to my place. You can come get your car later."

Charlie couldn't pass up her request. They got to her apartment just southeast of the New Hampshire side of the Memorial Bridge near Marcy and Atkinson. She had a really nice townhome type of place. Once inside, Charlie stood and looked around. Darlene kept a nice home; everything was in its place. Even the expressionist art hanging on the foyer wall next to the cat-wagging-its-tail clock was appealing.

"Oh that," she said. "It's a Twombly. I took a few art classes in college. You like it? Cy Twombly. He was a contemporary of Robert Rauschenburg. Most people see scribbles and graffiti, but you have to look more deeply into his art. He was really an American master of the mid-twentieth-century Abstract Expressionist movement."

"You never cease to amaze," Charlie blurted out, feeling drowsy.

"Follow me, sleepyhead," she laughed.

They wound their way from the foyer door toward a short hallway that headed toward one of two bedrooms. She stopped and turned around, facing Charlie.

"Stand right there," she said. "Don't go anywhere."

What a tease. This is gonna be great.

Just as soon as she disappeared, she returned, standing in front of him wearing nothing but a lavender bra and matching panties.

Charlie felt more awake . . . aroused. "You look . . . . fantastic."

She walked closer to him, standing mere inches from his frame.

"I have a question for you," he said.

"I'm all ears," she said.

"Why are you doing this to me? You're making it very easy for me. You could have any guy you ever wanted, right here, right now, at this very moment. Any guy, in the whole world, and you chose me."

"It's really very simple," she began. "I like you. You're mature. You're not some silly little horny idiot kid who drools all over me without really getting to sit down and know me. Usually, they say what they have to say to get into my pants. That's the only agenda they have. Someone like you, who actually plays things cool, and doesn't rush things. Now, there's a keeper. And I don't mind being the one to, um, make the move, if you know what I mean."

Charlie wondered if what she meant by playing it cool was forgetting to call her because of the demands of the investigation. He smiled to himself. He didn't realize the unintended consequences . . . benefits, of just doing his job.

Darlene reached back and unclasped her bra, and Charlie watched it flutter to the floor. Her eyes returned to his. Charlie was still fully clothed. She was getting serious, he thought. She grabbed his hands and placed them on her bare breasts.

Have I died and gone to heaven?

If he hadn't at that moment, he would be shortly.

CHAPTER 27

Charlie woke up the next morning in his bungalow's bedroom. After they'd slept together, Darlene drove him back across the bridge to the Tex-Mex place in Kittery to retrieve his Lincoln. The entire drive back to his place, he couldn't wipe the smile off his face. He woke up, refreshed, without the slightest sign of a hangover. He hoped he didn't make too much of a schmuck of himself. The sex was great and all, but in his heart, Charlie knew he liked her, but didn't *love* her. He made a mental note to see her again and talk about this—not from a place of regret, but a point of friendship.

If only the progress of the case could be this satisfying.

A shit, shower, and shave later, Charlie got on the phone and called Steve Richards. He not only felt refreshed this fine morning, he knew what to do next.

Later that day, in the late afternoon, Charlie drove the Lincoln to Luigi's Pizzeria in Haymarket Square, where Steve agreed to bring reports and statistics for all the murders that had taken place in southern New Hampshire around the time of Lyle Willems's murder. Charlie's subconscious nudged.

Time to broaden the scope.

He took a seat near the rear of the restaurant, and ten minutes later Richards showed up with a manila envelope. "It's all there," Richards said, once he'd ordered a beer—a regular Budweiser. He figured he was allowed since he promised his better half he'd curb the carbs and grease.

"Not sure why you need this shit. But there it is."

"Thanks, smart ass."

"Getting desperate, are we?"

"Rather not say."

"C'mon. What happened to the Great Charlie Redmond, outdoorsman extraordinaire?"

"Steve, you know as well as I do, there's just not a lot of evidence out there with this case. Very frustrating."

They ordered their food. A couple of deep-dish slices for Charlie and a small garden salad for Richards.

"We get these challenges all the time, Charlie," Richards said. "We've only got the resources that will allow us to solve what we can. C'mon, Charlie, you know there are tons of unsolved cold cases out there."

"Thanks for stating the obvious, dude."

Richards got more serious. "Look, Charlie, FYI, Liedeman and the others pored into this already, the other murders occurring around the time frame of the Willems murder. And nothing gave them an indication of any connection."

Charlie decided to stay mum about his meeting in Portland, and the bribe Liedeman took. "Yeah, I know, Steve. That's the crux of my frustration. No evidence."

Once their orders arrived, Charlie gave Richards a lengthy primer on the progression of the investigation. He told Richards about the events of the case thus far, of course leaving out what he promised Liedeman he would leave out, and selectively omitting his stint as a rogue cop in the SUV outside of the bakery recently.

Richards listened intently, nodding his head like he understood Charlie's logic. Pretty intriguing material, he thought, but much of it indefinite and ambiguous, essentially not offering much to advance the case.

The waitress came over and asked the men how the food was. Charlie didn't answer. Richards grimaced at his salad and said, "It's good, if you're a rabbit."

***

Charlie spent the next day at the bungalow reviewing the reports Richards gave him. In the year Lyle Willems was killed, no fewer than twenty murders occurred in the greater Portsmouth metropolitan area. In the two-month block that included his murder, there were four others. Portsmouth was no Boston. Five was a significant number, especially if there was at least one cold case among them. Turns out there were four such cases. One case was officially declared closed. Three hadn't been solved, in addition to Lyle's. Of the three cold-case murders that bookended the Willems murder, two had been killed within twenty-four hours of Lyle Willems. The other victim, a man named James Cross, had been killed two weeks before Lyle.

The two victims murdered within a day of Willems were named Margaret Martinez and Wendy Cushman. Charlie considered the stats for Martinez and Cross. Cross was African American, twenty-one years old, killed in a drive-by. Probably gang-related. Martinez was a twenty-two-year-old Latina, also shot to death, then decapitated, her body left outside a crack house.

Aside from ID-ing the victims, nothing else was done to investigate the cases. Sad, but perversely understandable.

Charlie looked at the stats surrounding the third murder. This murder wasn't like the other two. No compelling gang or proximate criminal connection. It wasn't exactly faceless like the other two. So, it immediately caught Charlie's eye. Wendy Cushman was killed in her apartment in southeast Portsmouth. The police reports described her as thirty, Caucasian, unemployed, dabbled in pot and coke. Police listed her brother, Peter Johns, who lived near Concord, as the one to ID her. The police report didn't suggest a possible reason for this murder. No betrayal of a dealer, or some similar reason. Still, there were no resources to keep this case warm, so it was on to the next case for the investigators.

Charlie studied the photo of the victim. Cushman had been killed on her bedroom floor, shot in the chest and face. In spite of the report's meager description, Charlie still thought drugs played more of a role. He also thought this was some type of machismo killing. (You screwed me, bitch, now your turn to die.) The crime-scene photos were troubling to Charlie. He never really got used to looking at them.

As an occupational hazard, there was a diminished emotional response a seasoned investigator would experience examining literally hundreds, thousands, of such photographs. But the progressive lack of sensitization to them was a quirk of the brain, a defense mechanism. It was one that would allow a detective to do his job without the cumbersome emotional investment. For this, Charlie was grateful. The crime scene photos were gruesome. Charlie struggled with the impulse to look away. Whatever the circumstances surrounding her death, *this was someone*. She mattered to at least one other person. She affected at least one other person. Murder was bad enough, but for a victim to die in such a violent manner, destroying whatever hope or desire she had in this life, there should have been motivation for an investigation to continue. There was always a reason for murder, especially a violent one. In some weird way, cases like this gave Charlie that motivation, even when hampered by an overwhelming lack of hard evidence. The motivation to solve a murder cold case, no matter how anonymous, no matter how notable, was always explained by Charlie by one simple fact: because *someone* was dead.

CHAPTER 28

Wendy Cushman had lived on Longmeadow Road in Portsmouth, just off Highway 1. Charlie took the highway toward that direction in the southern portion of the city. His destination bordered the Colonial Pines neighborhood, a working-class area in the southeastern corner of the city limits. Not a poverty-stricken grid, but populated by honest, hardworking New Hampshirites who were ambitious enough to move up the corporate and societal pecking order. It was a nice area with modest, mostly apartment-style living and affordable family restaurants, filled with parents, their children, and anybody else with dreams, passions, and a decent education upon which to build them. Charlie was familiar with the area, having investigated a couple of cases a few years back. Nothing major, on the scale of the Lyle Willems murder, at least. Just a couple of domestic spats that ended in assault convictions.

Charlie turned off the highway and drove to the address on the Cushman police report. He got out of his car and walked toward the front of the apartment complex located on Longmeadow. He found the super's dwelling and buzzed the corresponding number.

"Yes, may I help you?" a tinny-sounding voice said from the other end of the intercom.

"Is this Mr. Baker?" Charlie asked, using the name of the super from the police report, Bruce Baker.

"Yes, who's this?"

"It's the detective, Charlie Redmond. I'd like to ask you a couple of questions about Wendy Cushman. She lived here."

The door buzzed. Charlie saw that the complex was two stories, arranged in a quadrangle with a central courtyard. He found Bruce at his door, holding the hand of a small child.

Bruce was a slightly portly man in his mid-thirties, with oily black hair and graying temples. He wore a white T-shirt and baggy kelly-green sweatpants. He freed his right hand and held it out to shake Charlie's. "Hello. Nice to meet you. So, is this case finally opened up again? Honey, why don't you go back to your room, huh?" he said, as the girl scampered off.

Charlie shook Bruce's hand.

"Apologies . . . my daughter," Bruce said.

"Oh, no problem. Sometimes, I wish I had a kid myself," Charlie said, smiling. "My name is Charlie Redmond."

Bruce invited Charlie inside.

Charlie took a seat on the couch alongside a worn brown recliner. *Bruce probably used to give his gut a workout with cheap takeout and endless Budweisers.*

"So, I'm investigating another case besides Wendy Cushman. You may have heard about it. The one involving the murder of Lyle Willems."

"No, can't say I have," Bruce said, sitting down on his La-Z-Boy. "Could I interest you in a beer or somethin'?"

188

Charlie politely declined and said, "This has been a tough one for me to crack. I know a lot about the victim, Willems, but I'm investigating other events, murders, that took place around the time of Lyle Willems's murder to hopefully give me something to work with."

"So, you think that his murder may be connected in some way to Wendy's?" Bruce asked, returning to his Lay-Z-Boy with a Bud in his right hand.

"Well, I don't know. That's what I'd like to ask you about."

Bruce excused himself to check on his daughter, who seemed to be playing a video game in her bedroom.

God, I hope this isn't another wild goose chase. I can't take another loose end.

Bruce apologized for the interruption upon returning a few minutes later.

Charlie dove right in. "So, what was Wendy Cushman like as a tenant?"

"Well," Bruce began, sighing, "she was addicted to drugs. Wouldn't exactly call her a junkie, or anything. She was a really nice person. Really was. So sad about what happened to her."

"Yes, it was. Sounds as though you were affected by her."

"She was so charming, beautiful, full of life, tremendous potential. Even though she had no immediate family, she did have a brother, who really had nothing to do with her.

"She lived in the number right next to mine. I let her slide on rent from time to time. And I've kept it vacant out of respect."

"May I see it?"

The men left Bruce's apartment and went next door.

"I rented this space to her for three years prior to her death," Bruce said as he unlocked the door.

The inside of her small one-bedroom apartment was bare—just brown medium-pile carpeting and stucco drywall. A slight musty odor filtered through the rooms.

"This is it. When she could pay, I charged her four hundred dollars a month. She had trouble paying because she was always between jobs and such. All the other one-bedrooms are twice that," Bruce said.

Charlie nodded.

"Ever since she moved in here, she wanted to be independent, as she put it. She started going to school to get her certified medical assistant degree. She said she tried and failed as an actress in New York and had to move back to New Hampshire. But she also said she was willing to try anything to make good money, as she put it. Said she wanted to go into the health profession because she wanted to help people. But she could never get going with any of that, and I think she got depressed. Some of her so-called friends," Bruce made air quotes, "I think, led her down the wrong path, and she got hooked."

Charlie scanned the room a little longer. Tried to imagine her living within it. He didn't think it looked out of the ordinary. He wondered how long it took Bruce to clean things up after her brutal slaying.

"Why do you think that Wendy was killed?" Charlie asked.

"Mr. Redmond," Bruce began, "I have to tell you, whenever drugs are involved, it complicates so many things. I knew Wendy did drugs, so I would say that all of the events surrounding her death probably had something to do with her addictions. But, she was such a sweet woman. I could see she wanted to make something of herself from the moment she first asked for an apartment to rent here.

"But she got waylaid. She'd go for long periods when she wasn't staying in her apartment." Bruce walked around the room, shaking his head. "Little things, like her gradually losing weight, some white lies here and there about her comings and goings. She even had a boyfriend who would do what he could to watch out for her. His name was Murray. He came to me a few times when he couldn't find her and she wouldn't return his messages, and such.

"Then one day, Murray confirmed to me what I already knew. That Wendy was hooked on drugs. I felt so sorry for her. I kind of knew it was the end of the line for her. Ticking time bomb, and all that."

"You mean you were concerned that her drug addictions would lead to other problems, like prostitution, dealing, crime. Stuff like that?"

"Dunno. Guess that's what you have to figure out," Bruce said.

Chagrined, Charlie said, "I mean, generally. That illicit street drugs were Wendy's ultimate undoing, the reason she was murdered. The reason she got caught up in her unfortunate state and owed someone something, perhaps, paying the ultimate price. Feel me?"

"Sure, suppose. I mean, who knows? I don't claim to know all there is to know about the drug underworld and the criminal element that goes along with it." Bruce chuckled, nervous and a little emotional. "I'm a single dad with a little girl to raise. I want to protect her from all the shit that's out there. Seeing all that stuff on TV and on the Internet makes you think of all the worst, I guess. Drugs affected Wendy in such a way that she made bad decisions. I shudder just thinking about it."

Charlie walked over to the exact spot in the bedroom where she'd been murdered. He looked at Bruce. "What can you tell me about her boyfriend, Murray?"

"Murray Stevens," Bruce said. "I liked him. One of those gentle giant types. In his mid-thirties, stocky, athletic, but tenderhearted. From the moment Wendy moved into this complex, she started dating him. I'm a little embarrassed to admit that I wanted her to be happy. Kind of like the father she never had. I doted on her a little. I wanted things to work out real nice for those two."

Charlie nodded.

"They were great together, at first," Bruce continued. "Then Wendy's social life began to pick up with all the wrong types of people. She pretty much left Murray in the dust. She was moving too fast for him. I think he really loved her, but in the end, he knew he had to let her go. He's a good guy. He always kept an eye out for her, for the both of us. Still, he was just beside himself when Wendy was killed."

Bruce moved away from Charlie, back toward the apartment's living area. "Did the police ever consider him a suspect?" Charlie asked as he followed him.

"Oh my goodness, no. He was her boyfriend, then just her friend. He tried to look out for her, as I said. The only one who knew of her family, her brother, did everything he could to cooperate with the police before they stopped investigating the case."

Charlie and Bruce walked out of Wendy's old apartment. Bruce said, "Murray told me that just before she broke up with him, he knew that something dangerous was going on with her. He said that she was acting very strangely. That she'd be gone for days on end and would take forever to contact him. I cry every time I think about it. Maybe I could have done something to help her then, like stage an intervention."

Bruce began to sob and sniff. Charlie put his arm around Bruce. "Bruce, from what you told me, you did everything you could to help her. You forgave her rent on many occasions, supported and encouraged her relationship with Murray, and attempted to be the father she never really had. That's about as devoted as a guy could get without being a blood relative."

Bruce smiled at Charlie as he closed the apartment door behind them. "Hey, I just thought of something. I have a container with some of Wendy's stuff. Do you want to take a look?"

Charlie was surprised at the offer. Bruce knew that Charlie was an investigator.

Why didn't he tell me about this earlier?

Maybe Bruce was still being protective of his deceased honorary daughter's legacy. Maybe his emotions overcame him when he recounted Wendy's story to Charlie. Maybe he trusted Charlie now.

"Sure," Charlie said. "I'd love to take a look."

Bruce went inside his apartment and emerged from the guest bedroom with a cardboard box.

"I'm glad I'm showing this to you, Detective," he said. "I knew I'd kept this for a reason."

"How did you come to keep this box?" Charlie asked.

"When the cops investigated Wendy's murder, they discovered it in her bedroom closet. They looked through it and decided that it wasn't worth anything to them. They asked her brother if he wanted the things inside, but he declined. Guess I never really knew why I kept it, until now."

"Wendy's older brother, Peter Johns," Charlie pressed Bruce.

"Yeah, he was never there for her, the asshole. They had absolutely no relationship. Zero. I had no idea Wendy had a brother until Peter advised the police on what they could do with her body."

"And Murray? Did he want any of what was in this box?"

"He's looked through it. But he didn't want anything that was in there. Said keeping any of it would make him too emotional. I can understand that. Here, take it," Bruce said, handing the box to Charlie. "You can't keep any of it, for obvious reasons. But you're free to look through it, if that's okay."

Charlie thanked Bruce and headed toward the living room, where he placed the box on the coffee table. He rifled through pictures of Wendy, her friends, acting and cutting up in silly situations. She was a sight, with her friendly and attractive face. Some old newspaper clippings showed her taking the lead role in her high school production of *You're a Good Man, Charlie Brown*. Some trinkets and mementos mixed in with the photos and newsprint. Her actions portrayed in all of the pictures provided a glimpse into this woman in happier times, so much so that Charlie wished he could have been with her to experience them, before the tragedy. He sniggered at the thought. But she was compelling. Bruce's recollections only fueled Charlie's desire to find out if there was any connection with the Lyle Willems murder.

In the kitchen, Bruce was fixing an ice cream float for his daughter. He looked up at Charlie in the adjoining living room and called out, "Mr. Redmond, would you like a snack? Are you finished looking through all of that stuff of Wendy's?"

Charlie rose from the couch and yelled, a little preoccupied, "I'm gonna go outside for a sec and make a call."

"Oh, yeah, okay," Bruce said. He shrugged. "Sure, no problem."

Charlie couldn't wait to yank out his smartphone and dial Steve Richards. Once he got into his Lincoln, he made the call.

"Richards," Steve answered.

"Steve, it's Charlie. Hey, can you do me a quick favor?"

"Gee, dude, I don't know. How much is it worth to you? Shall I take a credit card . . . or will this be a debit transaction?" Richards said, chortling.

Here I am trying to gather pertinent information that could very well be critical to this case, finally, and this smart ass wants to dink around with me. Sheesh almighty!

"Jesus Christ . . . Listen," Charlie said. "I'm in the field at an apartment complex researching the Wendy Cushman case . . ."

"Oh boy, you're really asking for a special favor now. You tryin' to open that case up? Big-time request, my man," Richards interrupted, laughing harder. "Shall I rush out to you and pull down my pants for a quickie BJ?"

Charlie wasn't in the mood for Steve Richards's sophomoric behavior. Not when he was on the verge of discovering a possible link to all the crap he'd investigated so far.

"Motherfuck—" Charlie said, more tense.

Richards sensed Charlie's urgency and became earnest. "Okay, sorry, Charlie. I'm all ears."

"You sitting at your desk? Your computer?"

"You bet. What's up?"

"I need you to search this name, a guy by the name of David Medice. Not sure how it's pronounced. Med-*ice*, as in ice cubes?"

"Okay," Richards said. "I'll get back to you."

Charlie was on hold for a few before Richards got back on the line and said, "It's Med-*ees*, as in the long E, according to the file. Anyway, two popped up by that name, believe it or not. One of them is probably no use to you, unless there's a geriatric angle to the Cushman case. He's ninety years old this year."

Charlie rolled his eyes and said, "And the other?"

"He's forty and lives in the Portsmouth metro area, in Rye, on the coast. Has a rap sheet. Yada yada. What exactly are you looking for?"

"Drugs?"

"Nope," Richards said.

Charlie could practically see him shaking his big head on the other end.

"Nothing like that. Stuff like public indecency. Drunkenness. Could be something minor. Like he got fucked up at a party and made an ass of himself after mooning others with his. Or, could be something a little more significant. Never know," Richards continued.

Charlie said, "I was looking through some of Wendy Cushman's personal effects her apartment superintendent was showing me, and I discovered an item that looked like a business card among those things. A little odd, though. Unlike what you'd expect on business cards—one's name, position, contact info, what have you. This card only had his name on it."

"Well, like I said, the Medice we have here looks pretty criminally innocuous."

"Give me what you got," Charlie said.

"You got it, sir. Sorry about givin' you shit earlier. Like you said, I—"

Charlie clicked off before Richards could finish, and returned to Bruce Baker's apartment. Bruce was standing in the living area as though he were eagerly expecting Charlie's return.

"You left before I could ask you if you found anything interesting in that box," Bruce said.

"Nothing of serious note, but I did come across a card with a name on it. A guy by the name of David Medice. I had to call another detective back at the station to check it out. Apparently Wendy kept his card. Ever heard of him?"

Bruce shook his head. "Can't say I have. He could have been important to her on some level, but I probably never would have known about it. Wendy wasn't much into name-dropping."

Charlie thought for a second. "Well, I can always ask Murray about this. Could be something. Could be nothing. It could have been a card that Wendy accidentally placed in her box of stuff. Who knows?"

Bruce walked Charlie back to his Lincoln.

"I really appreciate your help today, Bruce."

"Have to admit," Bruce said, "I was a little nervous about it when you showed up. Guess I'm still a little protective of Wendy, even after all of this tragedy." Bruce smiled.

"Think nothing of it." Charlie got into his car and turned to Bruce to speak to him through the rolled-down driver's side window.

"I think Wendy's looking down at you and knows you're doing your part to avenge her murder," Charlie said, privately straining at the effort. He was never one for male bonding in situations like this.

Bruce choked back tears. "Yeah. Take care."

"Stay strong," Charlie said.

CHAPTER 29

Charlie didn't have to work hard to find Wendy's onetime paramour. Bruce simply gave him the address: 424 Jane Lane, in southern Portsmouth. Dusk settled in as Charlie rang the doorbell to the white McMansion.

When Murray came to the door, he looked just as Bruce had described him: thirty-five or so, stocky, slightly receding hairline.

"Murray Stevens?" Charlie asked.

"Yes?" he said.

"My name's Charlie Redmond. I'm an investigator, affiliated with the Portsmouth PD. Could I have a few minutes of your time?"

"Hey, I'm good," Murray said. "I paid all of my overdue speeding tickets last year."

Charlie gave a light smile at his joke. "Actually, I'm here because I'm investigating a murder. I obtained your name as a result of my investigation thus far. I'm trying to see if there's a link between the murder of Wendy Cushman and the murder I'm investigating."

Murray's expression changed from whimsical to serious.

No more crappy attempts at humor.

"Um, come on in," Murray said, motioning Charlie into the foyer and living room.

"Sure," Charlie said as he scanned his immediate surroundings. It was a guy's place, with dark, comfortable-looking leather furniture and brown thick-pile carpet. The adjoining dining room had one wall devoted to a curio cabinet of average height, filled with unused decorative dinner plates and goblets. From where he stood, Charlie could see stone tiles on the kitchen floor, and stainless steel appliances.

"Like a cold one?" Murray asked. "Just got through eating a small salad for supper. I usually have an after-dinner beer."

"Sure, do you have a light?"

"Of course, light beer is the only type I drink," Murray said. He explained to Charlie that he still considered himself fairly athletic although he had modest love handles and slightly thinning hair.

"I was just about to go for a run when you showed up."

A man after my own heart. He still considers himself physically fit while justifying his love of less-filling brews.

"Sorry about the intrusion," Charlie said, "but I came to ask you a couple of questions. I'm investigating a murder and I'm trying to find out if a one-time acquaintance of yours was connected to it in some fashion. Wendy Cushman."

Murray, still in the kitchen, clanged a couple of bottles together. "Yeah, it's been a hot minute since I've talked about Wendy to anyone. We were close at one time. What happened to her was tragic."

Murray lowered his voice as he returned to the living room, handing Charlie his lite beer. "But I'm glad that, at least, someone is looking into this case, because when Wendy was murdered . . ." He paused, seeming to reconsider what he was going to say. "Well, I'm just happy you're looking into it. I hope I can help in any way possible. Go ahead and take a seat."

Charlie sat on the leather sectional. Murray sat across from him in a matching recliner. He didn't prop up his legs, but opted to rock back and forth, taking an occasional swig of beer. Charlie spied Murray's shirt, an athletic jersey that read WILDCATS HOCKEY.

"You played hockey for UNH?"

"Just one year, my freshman year. Then I injured my MCL, one too many times," Murray said, shaking his head. "It was too bad, because I was having a blast. The season I played we made it to Division One playoffs."

"Absolutely," Charlie said, with a wide smile. "One of Coach Bowes's final years. You guys went nine and three that season."

"Whoa! You know that? Cool!"

"Love hockey. Never good enough to play it after my high school years, though."

"Sweet," Murray said, as he finished his first bottle in no time flat. "Want another?"

"OK, if you don't mind, I'll. . . "

Charlie nodded as Murray went back to the kitchen to retrieve his second. He then sat back down in the recliner. This time he was a little more comfortable, with the chair, his second beer, and with Charlie. He propped his legs up.

"So, I understand you were Wendy's boyfriend at some point," Charlie said, trying to catch Murray off guard.

"Yep, we were an item, I guess you'd say, for a couple years. We started dating not long after she moved to the

Portsmouth area. We actually met at a party way before the drugs and all that. Of course, her drug use led to our breakup."

"That's too bad."

"She was really great to be around. Really sweet."

"But then her lifestyle spun out of control, right?"

"Believe me, I wanted us to stay together. But she got into coke, mostly. She stopped calling me, honoring appointments and things. I would call out her lies, and we would argue. It wasn't good. You know, it's the classic storyline, cliché actually. Beautiful, naïve girl moves into town with all of these dreams and ideals. Said she even was a struggling actress before moving here. Then she gets swept away into this abyss of negativity. Pathetic."

"How long after you two broke up was she killed?"

"About a year."

Charlie knew he'd have to be gentle with the next question. "Were there any other men in her life after she broke up with you? Anyone she may have had any relationship with, not necessarily a romantic one?"

"To my knowledge she was never involved with anyone after me, even in a romantic context. I don't see how, really, unless he used drugs, too. She was with other men, hung out with them, but hanging out with other men isn't the same as being in love with them."

Murray was sanguine in his comments to Charlie. But he was willing to tell his story. *Perhaps he was looking for catharsis. Still searching for it.*

Murray continued. "Her personality was a magnet. Strangers approached her constantly. As she spent less time with me, she would spend more time with other guys. But those were merely encounters. She was married to her addictions."

"Well, like I said earlier, I'm not actually investigating Wendy's death specifically," Charlie said. "I'm investigating the murder of a man named Lyle Willems and a possible connection to Wendy's murder. Have you ever heard that name? Lyle Willems?"

Murray seemed circumspect. "Yes, he was a big fish in the medical device industry, the Bill Gates of med devices. In my line of work, everyone knew about him. Did Wendy actually have something to do with his murder?"

"Not entirely sure. But they were murdered on the same day."

Murray shook his head in disbelief. "Well, this isn't a big city, but were there any other murders within the twenty-four hours of Wendy's?"

"Only one. I've looked into it, also."

"Do you see a connection there?"

"Not aware of any, yet."

Murray became bolder and said, "I don't think the cops ever had any interest in finding Wendy's killer. You know? I mean, to them, she was insignificant. No immediate family, except a brother she told me about, maybe once. No money. Whatever. I don't think they gave a crap."

"Yeah, I think you're probably right," Charlie said. He sighed. "Let's talk about the drugs. Do you think that drugs directly led to Wendy's murder?"

"Yep, I mean, probably," Murray said, not as cynical now. "I'm pretty sure that Wendy was deeper into drugs and her lifestyle than she let on. Whenever I actually did get a chance to talk to her, confront her, about this, she just blew me off. It got worse and worse with her. I couldn't control her, stop her from making the biggest mistake of her life. I think that her behavior finally went too far. In the world she made for herself, she probably ticked off the wrong person, and . . ." He paused and swallowed. "Someone killed her."

Charlie sensed Murray's growing unease. "I really appreciate your help. I'm sure it's hard bringing all this stuff up, all over again."

"Thanks," Murray said. "As I said, I'm glad you're revisiting the case, even if it's not your primary focus."

Charlie decided to press on. "Have you ever heard of someone named David Medice?"

"David Medice," he mused. "No, doesn't ring any bells. Why?"

"Well, it's come up in my investigation."

"Who's he?"

"I don't know. Right now, it's just a name I've come across while researching Wendy's murder. I've become familiar with the name from old Portsmouth PD reports." Charlie didn't want to tell Murray about the actual circumstances surrounding his discovery of David Medice. How Bruce Baker showed him a box of Wendy's very personal effects. He didn't want Murray to know that some nosy detective was able to look into the life of his dead girlfriend. So he fed Murray a line of police report crap in hopes he wouldn't question it further. He didn't.

"I hope you find him," Murray said, "if he had anything to do with Wendy's death."

"Actually, it'll be easy to find him. He lives in Portsmouth. Whether or not he had anything to do with her death, that's the big question."

Looking relieved, Murray got up and started for the kitchen. He turned toward Charlie and held out his bottle, suggesting to Charlie, *want another?*

Charlie politely declined and told Murray he had to leave. He'd come to get some straight answers from Murray, to see if there was a connection to Lyle Willems's murder, to find out if he knew David Medice. They walked to the foyer.

"Must be cool to be a PI," Murray said. "Makes great TV. I love those types of shows."

Charlie smiled. "I'm actually retired from the department. Every now and again, if there's a cold case they just can't crack, they call me." Charlie paused for a second to study Murray's face, looking for concern. He didn't find it. He continued. "Too young for social security, but the business the department generates for me supplements the pension a little. Not as glamorous as you're thinking, probably."

Is this guy looking for a bromance?

"Well, it was really cool to talk with you," Murray said. "If you have further questions, don't hesitate to seek me out." He wrote down his number on a piece of paper.

Charlie took the paper and started to exit, then turned around. "You mentioned earlier your line of work. What do you do? Do you work from home, Murray?"

"No, I work at a local Internet startup, New England Science Today. It's a science and tech newsgathering service. Like I told you earlier, it was next to impossible for anyone working in this industry to be unaware of Lyle Willems. Our operation was a little bumpy initially, but once we got some venture capitalists on board with deep pockets and a little faith, we were on our way. We're doing pretty well now with fundraising rounds. I smell an IPO pretty soon," Murray said, rapping his fist against the wooden table next to the door. "We were one of the few that survived when the dot-com bubble burst. I'm pretty stoked for the future of the company."

Impressive. Mental note: research this guy's startup.

Murray showed Charlie out. It had been a productive day for Charlie. He got into his Lincoln and headed back to his place. He thought about everything he had learned so far. He thought about the new pieces of information he learned. About how those things have influenced his investigation, taken it in directions he didn't anticipate. But was Charlie ultimately any closer to the truth? He discovered new things about Lyle Willems and Wendy Cushman, but at the end of the day, how did they relate to each other? Exasperated and a little fatigued, he headed north on Highway 1. He smiled as he got his first glimpse of the Piscataqua River. It seemed from his initial, cursory look at the other murders within the twenty-four-hour period of Lyle Willems's murder that Wendy's killing was the only one that could possibly be connected. But, as was the norm with everything he'd learned so far, there simply wasn't evidence to connect them.

Back at his bungalow, Charlie had more time to relax and think. Now he felt even less sure of a connection between the two murders. They just seemed to be so disparate. He decided he wouldn't tell Carla about these new developments. Not yet, anyway. Maybe she'd think that he was still grasping at straws. He would have to be sure of his information. He didn't want to disappoint her with news of more loose ends. However, there was a lot of information. Charlie couldn't ignore that.

He also couldn't ignore where his subconscious was taking him. From Brenda Turner to the massage parlor to the killing of a young, impressionable woman named Wendy Cushman. Charlie knew he had to keep digging to pull these things, these ideas, these people, together. Perhaps David Medice would be the catalyst. A phone call to him would be all that it would take to get things going . . . again.

CHAPTER 30

Charlie felt a pressure in his chest, a pastiness in his mouth. *It wasn't your fault. . . .* His phone buzzing on the nightstand table snapped him awake.

"Charlie," Carla's voice said, "I hope I didn't interrupt you. But I was wondering, would you like to go hiking with me?"

Charlie quickly came to. "Hiking? Like right now?"

"Yes, right now. Remember how you said that no matter how the investigation goes, you need to stay fit for your extreme hiking vacation? Plus, I'm thinking you could probably use a little break."

"Yes!" Charlie said. "I mean yes—yes, Carla. Why don't I come over to your place and meet you?"

"Sounds great," Carla said. Charlie thought he could detect a smile. "You know where I live."

***

A few minutes later, they were on their way to Pawtuckaway State Park, which featured a mix of moderate and challenging trails.

"I really love it out here," Charlie said to Carla, as the two passed the Pawtuckaway Lake to their east on the way to the trail. Charlie didn't tell her he was taking her to the South Ridge Trail—not super challenging, but not a cakewalk, either. "Just another venue for me to get out and think."

Charlie parked the Lincoln at the trailhead, and he and Carla geared up. He looked at her as they began the initial ascent, seeing she was a little short of breath. "You okay?"

"Me? Of course," she said. "I can handle this."

"I could've taken you on a more challenging course. Want to try one?"

Carla kept walking, a little more slowly, shooting him a cold look that said *I don't need you to hold my hand, Charlie.*

They reached a plateau about a third of a mile in, and Carla found a formation to rest on. Charlie walked over to her and knelt down.

"We should turn back," he said. "You're a little out of breath."

Carla just looked at the ground, seemingly a little embarrassed. When he offered to carry her backpack, she just nodded.

"Seriously, now, Carla," Charlie said. "Why'd you call me up wanting to hike all of a sudden?"

"No particular reason," she said, between deep breaths. "Guess I wanted to tell you how much I appreciated all you're doing. By doing something with you that you liked to do."

Charlie felt gratified. It wasn't enough for her to pick up the phone and thank him—she'd actually taken the initiative to do something her body would be sorry for the next day.

Carla said, not as winded, "Looks like we're a quarter mile to the parking lot."

Charlie looked at her and smiled. It was his turn to share. "When I hike these trails, it gives me time to reflect on the things that are most important to me," he said. "One of the first trails I hiked in Massachusetts when I was in college was with my first crush, Jenna Walsh.

"She was really into hiking and mountaineering. Probably nowhere near as athletic as you, though," Charlie said to Carla, smiling. "We met at a college social and immediately hit it off because, well, we had this interest in common, for the most part."

There was a feeling of discomfort again, and Charlie wished he had his headband on, to cover the sweat forming on his forehead.

"Charlie, you don't have to tell me this. . . ."

"When we were seniors in college, I qualified for this hiking competition in Utah, The Maze, in the Canyonlands National Park. I had to do it—alone. I had to be the white knight, to go and kick everyone else's ass. I was either too proud or too stupid to ask for emotional support."

Carla's eyes grew wide. She knew where this was headed.

"So I competed. And on the second day of the competition, I got a call from Jenna's mom. Jenna had gone to a convenience store for some milk. As she was about to leave, the place was held up. Those two fuckers came in and just started shooting. Jenna was caught in the crossfire and shot in the back of the head."

Carla looked at Charlie with tears in her eyes.

"She was brought to the hospital but was essentially DOA. I returned to Boston as soon as I could, but I never got to see her."

"Oh Charlie . . ."

Charlie knew what Carla was about to say. That what happened wasn't his fault. That he had nothing to do with her death. That things like this happen, of course, for a reason. But no soothing words, no reassurance on the ways of fate, no rational, measured tones of comfort from a friend, could simply put an end to how Charlie felt about the episode.

The fact was, what happened to Jenna had always affected Charlie, and, for all he knew, the way he'd lived his life ever since. Charlie had to live with the guilt of being selfish, with the guilt of placing himself before the person he loved. He had to live with the pain of losing the first love of his life. He had to live with the fear of losing another if he ever felt as close to that person as he did with Jenna. Maybe that's why he never could be as intimate with Carla as he could have been with Rebecca, the first woman he married. Maybe it had nothing to do with sex, but everything to do with the fear of getting close enough, just enough, to get burned in the end.

Charlie was able to rationalize a one-night drunken, debauched sexual tryst with a corporate secretary because he felt no psychological bond. Carla was a different story. Her existence in Charlie's life transcended mere resemblance to Jenna. He actually cared about her emotional welfare. Fucking her—even if it were a mercy fuck—would be wrong.

Charlie knew Carla needed to heal, just like he did. Her journey as an author was no different than Charlie's search for a trustworthy soul. They were both still navigating these challenges, their interactions with each other a work in progress. In the sport of love and relationships, they were playing the long game.

Pretty ironic, Charlie thought. Ironic that his pushing Jenna away for what he thought was her own good was the worst thing that could have happened to her. It seemed as though he should be able to fall in love again, get closer to that person so that nothing like this would ever happen to her. But life didn't work that way. It was much more complex. He still had yet to figure it all out.

"That's okay, Carla. You don't have to say anything. It was a long time ago."

They reached the parking lot and stood, facing each other.

"I sought you out because I wanted to do something principled," Carla said. "You know, righteous. That's probably why you wanted to be a detective. Correct? Because, after what happened to Jenna, you wanted to do something moral, something honorable?"

Charlie said, "I became a detective because I needed a job. After Jenna, I was lost. Didn't do anything for a long time. Finally, Steve Richards approached me and started giving me work, a purpose."

"Steve must've known you could handle situations like that," Carla said.

"Sure, I know. But I also think that he trusted me. He'd known me for a long time. He knew in his own crazy way that he'd be helping me out. So, I got into it, this line of work, and here we are." Charlie flashed a quick smile and a laugh. "It's also why I'm not clear across the other side of the world hiking at this very moment."

"Yes, I know, and I'm very fortunate you decided to stay this time," she said.

The two looked at each other.

"Come here," Carla said.

"Closer?"

"Yes, here."

Charlie leaned closer to her and she kissed him on the cheek. She whispered to Charlie, "I'm glad you agreed to take me with you today, on such short notice. Not sure my body will be so appreciative tomorrow, though."

Charlie savored the moment and smiled, not wanting to drive her home.

***

Charlie got up the next morning and went out for a run. More hill work, and an extra kilometer. Charlie loved it. There was something different about this morning's training, something positive. He had Carla to thank for it. He ran for at least a couple of hours, finishing more motivated than he'd been in days. His mind was clear once he came back to the bungalow. He had to stay in shape for his eventual extreme hiking challenge in New Zealand. He showered, dressed, made coffee and sat down in the living room. He pulled out David Medice's number from his notes and dialed it.

"Yeah?" a male voice answered.

Excellent.

"David?" Charlie said.

"Yeah?" David Medice said, sounding a little pissed.

Probably didn't recognize the number on his caller ID.

"David, this is Charlie Redmond. I'm an investigator."

A quick silence. "Can I help you?"

"Maybe. I thought I could meet you in person."

"What's this about?" Medice said, sounding a little more irritated than worried. As if to say, *I didn't do anything. . .*

"I'm investigating a murder. And, wouldn't you know it, your name came up."

"What murder?"

"Well, it's probably better to meet with you in person to discuss this. I promise it won't take long, like literally, a couple of questions," Charlie said, trying to reel Medice in.

Another pause, then Medice said, "Okay, sure, but not today. I'm busy today. How about Sunday, tomorrow?"

"That'll do nicely," Charlie said.

"Why don't you stop by midafternoon, around two. Do you know where I live?" Medice asked.

"Sure," Charlie said. "Right off Wedgewood Road in Gosling Meadows."

"How'd you know that? I'm not even listed."

"You've got a criminal record."

"Yeah, barely," Medice said.

"Barely equals yes," Charlie said, and he hung up.

***

Sunday afternoon Charlie took US Highway 4 to the Gosling Meadows neighborhood and the address Steve Richards gave him. The entire trip, Charlie thought about how David Medice could fit into this entire puzzling Lyle Willems case. He hoped he wasn't being led down another investigatory rabbit hole. Following all clues is what an excellent investigator did. He chased down every lead, every clue, even the most infinitesimal one, because an experienced detective had to stay one step ahead in the game. But it was a gray area. Chase too many crappy leads, then you're a fool for a detective.

Charlie knew it was entirely possible that David Medice could have nothing to do with the case. But what if he were the missing link? What if Lyle Willems had a drug habit and owed a supplier money? Could Wendy Cushman and David Medice have played a role? Wendy was into drugs, and Lyle was cloak and dagger about his lifestyle. At autopsy, according to the police reports, Lyle Willems had no evidence of drugs in his system, only alcohol, but that didn't mean he'd never used. And could there be a connection between Wendy Cushman, the massage parlor, and David Medice? The massage parlor where Lyle Willems may or may not have taken part in a lesbian sex romp?

Jesus Christ, who the fuck knows?

It could be something, anything, or nothing. As Charlie thought more and more about this, the more confused he got. First of all, evidence was scant. Secondly, he was thinking himself in circles trying to make sense of it all.

Maybe Steve Richards was right. Maybe I'm pursuing a useless hunch.

Charlie's smartphone rang: an unidentified number. "Charlie Redmond."

"Mr. Redmond, it's Bruce Baker. Wendy's landlord. Mr. Redmond, I'm calling because you remember when I went to the bedroom and brought out the box with all of Wendy's things?"

"Yes," Charlie said. Of course he remembered.

"Well, that's not really why I'm calling."

Both Charlie and Bruce knew that's *exactly* why he was calling, but neither confessed to that fact. It was sort of like small talk, a segue to something even more important. At least, that's what Charlie thought.

"I found something else on the closet floor next to where I keep her box, and I never noticed it before. I think you should come over and check it out."

"Believe it or not, I'm near your apartment. I'll just turn off on 95 and double back," Charlie said. "I'll be right there."

Charlie found Bruce waiting in the apartment quadrangle's portal. Once inside, Bruce disappeared into his bedroom. His daughter was asleep in his recliner.

"I found this when I was straightening things out in the closet," he said when he came back. He handed a letter-sized envelope to Charlie.

"I honestly don't know how I missed this the other day. I have to confess, I did open it up and take a look. Hopefully, this'll help you pursue justice for Wendy."

Charlie thanked Bruce for his vigilance. He sat down at the living room coffee table and poured out the contents: two typed letters, on high-quality paper, each about three-quarters of a page. All had the same signature, in black ink:

You are my world,
David

Charlie read the letters over.

Slowly, carefully, you entered my heart./Your love spread through me./Along my path, in my sights./Now, in every direction, there is you—just you./There's a storm of emotion in the rise and fall of my breath./The beating of my heart, it shakes my chest./What madness, what obsession . . . /What can I say of my state now?/My heart, my soul, my whole world/All my desire is you—just you . . .

Whenever I look at you, I gather the ideas/that you were made before the flowers/and then God copied on you to make the roses./Why are you so perfect, God only knows . . . /Your beautiful eyes and breathtaking hair/Captivated my gaze, so long as I stare/If given a wish, my wish would say/I wish for your wish to come true today. . . .

Both were love letters to Wendy. In spite of the prose's intensity, there was a certain pleasantness to David Medice's words. He truly seemed to love her, and believed that one day they would be together.

"Does this information give you a helpful lead? You can take them if you'd like." Bruce asked, yearning to play Charlie's earnest assistant.

"Yes, Bruce, thanks for this. In fact, I was just on my way to pay David Medice a visit."

"Well, good luck," Bruce said. "And be careful."

***

Charlie pulled off Highway 4 at a convenience store on his way to David Medice's address. His mouth was dry. He needed to wet it, although he wished he could do so with a stiff vodka. He would have to settle for bottled water instead.

218

After purchasing the water, he returned to his car. Before cranking the ignition on the Lincoln, Charlie sat and stared ahead. He looked at the envelope containing the letters, sitting on the passenger seat. He decided that he wouldn't take them into David's house when he paid a visit. He wasn't ready to show him the information he had on him. He was going to feel this guy out, divine the info out of him.

Charlie exited onto Wedgewood from the highway and turned into Medice's driveway. He lived in a modest one-story home with a decent-sized yard. Working class, typical of the properties on this street in the Gosling Meadows area of the city, although the neighborhood housed its share of more expensive homes inhabited by professionals of many stripes. Medice lived in this community, which was situated just northeast of the city's airport, by way of the Piscataqua River.

Charlie got out and walked toward Medice's residence and climbed the slightly rotted wooden steps to the front door. Before he could knock, the front door swung open and Medice stood at the threshold, all five-foot-nine of him. At just forty years old, his five o'clock shadow, overweight build, thin-rimmed spectacles, and balding salt-and-pepper pate made him look older than Charlie.

Although he was expecting Charlie, he didn't exactly dress for the occasion. He looked as though he'd just got up from pulling a Saturday all-nighter, whatever *that* involved. Charlie studied Medice. He was standing at the door's threshold, dressed in a sweat-stained undershirt and red cloth robe. His right hand cradled the front doorknob. His left held a drink. He let out a burp.

"You must be Charlie Redmond, one of Portsmouth's finest," Medice said.

Charlie nodded.

"I work in television myself, reality TV. I actually had a production company in New York before I came here a couple of years ago."

Charlie stood at the door with a faint smile, waiting for the guy to ask him inside.

"Oh, my bad," Medice said, motioning his left hand toward Charlie, careful not to spill his booze. "Why don't you come in?"

Charlie entered the claustrophobic living room, where trade magazines and DVDs littered the floor and coffee table. Charlie wanted to ask Medice if he'd ever considered Netflix but held off.

"Sorry for the mess," Medice said, seemingly a little embarrassed. He shoved some of the magazines around to allow a clearing for Charlie to sit on the loveseat. Medice plopped down on his recliner.

"Do you still do reality television?" Charlie asked.

"Are you suggesting that I'm a has-been?" Medice asked, with a slight grin.

"Well, you said you *had* a production company before you moved here from New York. Just putting two and two together."

Medice sipped his drink. "How perceptive you are, Detective. I don't have a company, *per se*. But my feelers are out there. I sustain myself by submitting scripts for commercial spots here in New Hampshire, local stuff. It only takes one script to get back in the thick of things, you know. Yeah, New York's a competitive place. My company had to fold. If you can't make it there, well . . ."

Medice looked at the floor for a second or two, as if he were contemplating his recent failures, his current lot in life, then he looked at Charlie and said, "Could I get you a drink? Mine's a vodka cosmopolitan."

Of course, it is.

"That's okay. I'm fine," Charlie said.

My vodka moment passed.

Medice rearranged his balls as he sat, took another drink, and said, "So, what would you like to know?"

"Well, for starters, are you married?" Charlie asked, wondering what type of woman would actually fall for someone like this man.

"Divorced. Three times," Medice said, as if he were bragging.

Charlie nodded his head, looked around the guy's disheveled home, and returned his gaze toward Medice.

You silly sonofabitch. Here you sit in your ratty recliner, dressed like some college fraternity rebel without a clue, nursing who knows how many drinks within the past twenty-four hours, coming across as some big shot who revels in past glories because it makes you think you're something special for surviving it all. This guy.

But was he bizarre enough to commit a heinous murder? Perhaps two? Charlie couldn't figure out the answer just yet.

"So, who was killed?" Medice asked.

"Two persons, actually," Charlie answered. "One of them was named Wendy Cushman. Tell me, did you know anyone by that name?"

Medice took a final swig of his vodka mixed drink from the glass he was holding, twisted his face, and cocked his neck, as if to show Charlie he was really thinking hard about the question, and then said, "Nope."

"You sure? She was a struggling young woman who was willing to try anything to make money after she moved to Portsmouth. She didn't live too far from here."

"Could be any sad-sack bitch. Why are you asking me about her?"

"Wendy Cushman had a contact named David Medice."

"Nope. Can't say I've ever heard of her. It wasn't this David Medice, by God," he said, pointing to his chest.

"Really," Charlie said. "You've never heard the name Wendy Cushman."

Medice wasted no time in answering again, this time without pissy theatrics. "Like I told you. No." A pause. "Who was the other person killed?"

"Lyle Willems."

"The CEO guy?"

Charlie nodded.

"Yes, I remember seeing it on the news. They never caught the dude who killed him?"

"No, they never did catch the dude . . . or woman."

"Are they connected?" Medice asked.

"You mean is there a connection between Lyle Willems and Wendy Cushman?" Charlie said.

"Yes."

"I'm not sure," Charlie conceded.

"Well, I never met Lyle Willems," Medice said. "I read about him. Fascinating guy. You would think that I would have crossed paths with him. From what I understand, he was a media whore. Putting on functions with entertainers and politicians and such. I would have loved to have worked with him."

"So, you're sure you've never met him?"

"Like I said. No, I mean, yes, I never met him. But I would have loved to have met him."

Charlie examined Medice.

Calm, practically stolid. Keeping the conversation going for the sake of conversation. Not one ounce of nervousness in him. Could be a front for self-imposed isolation or guilt.

Charlie looked at the walls again. He didn't see any photos with Medice's likeness. There were many other pictures of people—local media celebrities and the like—but none with him. Charlie decided to press the issue.

"Don't see any pics of you around here," Charlie said, taking in the photos on the walls. "Just a lot of local media celebrities."

"You won't. Having pictures of myself would make me sad. I don't want to be sad, Mr. Redmond. I don't like to have constant reminders of the days that were. Gotta live in the here and now."

"Sure."

Charlie informed Medice of the day that Lyle Willems and Wendy Cushman were killed. He asked Medice if he could recall what he was doing that week.

Again, Medice scrunched his nose and made a sucking sound with his teeth. "Boy, that was such a while ago. Let me think. I'm pretty sure I was in Boston for a week or two, trying to line up some business."

If this were any other period in the investigation, Charlie would have stopped his questioning. But he knew he had to keep the pressure on this guy. This cool-as-a-cucumber prick seemed to know more than he was letting on. Charlie didn't want to spring the letters on him. He knew he'd be able to turn this lead into something tangible, something that could blow this baby completely wide open. His subconscious prodded him: *You know you can do this. You know you can get what you want, what you need, from this jerk.*

Charlie listened to himself and soldiered on. "You think you can prove that . . . that you were out of the city when you said you were?" He was still employing tact, although Charlie hoped that Medice was too smug with himself to notice his slight frustration.

"I think I can find my boarding pass receipts," Medice said. "Want me to look around?"

"No, not now," Charlie said. He didn't want Medice to get too concerned, too worried about things. This was a slow burn.

Charlie gave Medice his card and stood. "Here, if you find those tickets or boarding passes, contact me. I really appreciate your help today. I know you had to get out of bed and all . . ."

Medice offered a smirk at Charlie's jab but managed deference as Charlie got up to leave. "You got it." He was ready to close the front door when Charlie abruptly turned around.

"Oh, and by the way," Charlie asked, "what reality shows are you most famous for producing?"

Medice let out an exasperated sigh resembling an equine whinny. "Um, a reality show for MTV about a decade ago called *Bling Me Out.*"

Charlie nodded and smiled. "Hmm, never heard of it. Thanks again for your time." Then he left.

CHAPTER 31

Charlie got home that evening just in time for the sunset. He wished he had the time and patience to take in its rich hues of red and orange. Instead, he brooded about the case and the day's developments. He also considered Medice and why he wasn't telling the truth, about why Medice needed to feign ignorance with the people in this investigation Charlie may have contacted.

That woman from the massage parlor reacted the same way. David Medice, Wendy Cushman, Lyle Willems, and the massage parlor, they intersect, but how, dammit? What am I missing?

The sun had already set. Dusk. As Charlie sat in the driveway, facing his one-car garage that was too narrow for his big boat, his smartphone startled him.

"Yep," he answered, deciding to take a chance on an unknown number.

"Yeah, hello, Mr. Redmond . . . Charlie. It's David Medice."

Charlie straightened up.

"I found my boarding passes. Yes, I was in Boston that week."

Charlie remained silent.

"I'm sorry. Couldn't hear you. Did we break up?" Medice said.

"No, we didn't break up. I heard you."

"Well, I have the tickets, too. I'm sure you'll want to see those, as well, right? You want to come back by—"

"Too late tonight," Charlie interrupted. "I'll contact you when I want to see them."

"Oh, okay, then."

"Thanks for calling me with that information. I appreciate it, David."

"Yeah, sure. And I wanted to let you know that *Bling Me Out* is on DVD. I can send it to you if you'd like. You told me you hadn't heard of it. Just an FYI. Now you can catch it at your convenience."

Charlie rolled his eyes.

Medice suddenly found the tickets and passes? And had the show on DVD? Who the hell still watches DVDs?

"Yeah, I'll have to check it out," he said, exasperated, before clicking off the call.

He finally got out of the car and walked toward the bungalow. He thought some more. *Now, this guy Medice is calling, practically begging me to examine the proof I wanted. It seemed a little too tidy, too convenient, his calling that same night, right after I left his place. He suddenly found the tickets and passes? Come on. Although, if the tickets were legit, then does his behavior suggest that Medice is innocent of her murder, but he still may have known Wendy?*

Once inside, Charlie pulled up the Internet Movie Database on his computer. Apparently Medice was telling the truth about his relative professional inactivity the past few years. The last show he produced, *Bling Me Out*, was canceled four years ago.

Charlie scrolled down the list of other shows, listed in chronological order by year of production: *Spring Break Showdown*, *Don't Play Me*, and Medice's most recent association, a short-lived sketch comedy program from a couple of years ago cheekily named *Flaccid*. He had an idea. He looked up Wendy Cushman. (He implicitly hoped that Wendy had nothing to do with a program named *Flaccid*.) There were actually three women by that name presented. He clicked on the first one. She was active in bit roles as a character actress in 1940s-era B-movies. Her death was listed in 1979. Charlie clicked on the second Wendy Cushman. There was only one listing for her, a role in an early 1950s television variety show, one of those whose sponsor's name was also in the title. She apparently wasn't terribly successful. The database listed her death in 1985.

Then he clicked on the final Wendy Cushman. No picture of her.

Of course.

Just like the previous entry, this Wendy Cushman had only one credit to her name. More significant, however, was the fact that, of the three Cushmans, her credit was the only one from the twenty-first century, a small part in a reality show called *The Big Payday*. No birth date or date of death. This was probably the Wendy Cushman who was murdered. This was the Wendy Cushman Charlie was interested in. Had to be. But the information in the database didn't help him much beyond its listing.

Keep looking, Charlie's subconscious urged. He undressed down to his boxers, streamed on the stereo Fleetwood Mac's *Bare Trees* (the only album they made that mattered), and took out a cold Bud Light. He sat down and closed his eyes.

***

The next morning, Charlie woke up, showered, dressed, and called Randi Martin, an acquaintance and former client with whom he maintained professional contact. She worked at MTV Networks in New York as vice president of their reality television and documentary programming. Charlie had worked with her when he was in Boston, where she was an executive at one of the local TV stations. There had been a security breach of sorts when the station's offices were broken into and advance copies of a multipart documentary project were stolen. Charlie was hired to hunt down the bad guys. He was successful. The perps were higher-ups from a rival station trying to undermine her station and come out on top in the ratings. They ended up serving time in white-collar minimum security. Randi went on to bigger and better things.

She was beautiful, ambitious, and still on the market. Too bad Charlie never slept with her. He may have considered it, but business always got in the way, like now.

"Randi Martin's office," her secretary said.

"Hello. Charlie Redmond calling for Randi."

A minute passed: "Well, well. Charlie Redmond, Detective Superman. To what do I owe the pleasure?"

"Oh, believe me," he said, "the pleasure's all mine. How are you, Randi?"

"I'm well. It's been a while, Charlie. Busy, as usual. You know, I was thinking about you the other day."

"Were you taking a bubble bath?"

She laughed her special laugh, magnetic and funny. He was honored she took so much pleasure in his comments. She knew exactly how to engage Charlie.

"Could you do me a favor?"

"Absolutely, my Superman."

"I'm working on a case. I need to find out if a reality actress was in or an extra in one of the shows on your network a few years ago."

"Sure, what were the shows you were thinking of?"

"*Bling Me Out, Don't Play Me*, and *The Big Payday*."

"Well, *Bling Me Out* was a huge show for the network. Who's the actress?"

"Wendy Cushman."

"Is this about the guy who directed most of the episodes in the series?"

"No, I'll have to fill you in later."

"No, you won't."

"Okay, you're probably right."

She laughed that loud, engaging laugh that seemed to keep all invitations open for a follow-up.

Charlie said good-bye, hung up, and called information for Laconia, New Hampshire. Charlie was familiar with the lakeside town, having hiked around the junctions of the two lakes, Winnipesaukee and Winnisquam, years ago. Laconia was situated about thirty miles to the north of Concord. It had its picturesque parts, and much of the community had a historic feel. Incorporated in the mid-nineteenth century, the town was a manufacturing center in the state, home to textile, rail, and lumber industries. Over the last fifty years or so, the history of the small city became secondary to its status as a sleepy bedroom community, about as milquetoast and free of drama worthy of the origin of its name, the Greek region of Laconia. The town was also the most recent address of Wendy Cushman's brother and closest known family member, Peter Johns. Charlie was able to obtain Johns's address and phone number. He got in his Lincoln and headed northwest from Portsmouth.

Charlie took State Highway 16 toward Milton, driving parallel to the Maine-New Hampshire border. Charlie was anticipating the drive. Not only was he extremely close to finding out Wendy Cushman's possible connection with the Lyle Willems murder, he was looking forward to revisiting a part of the state that was always special to him. Usually not one for camping, the richly sylvan corridor was a favorite of Charlie's on long hiking excursions and protracted camping trips. He spent time as an adolescent on trips to the region for hiking, school trips, and numerous orienteering exercises. Although he had a mandate to get to Laconia as soon as he could, he pulled off the road a few times to indulge himself in scenic parts he hadn't visited in years.

Back on the road, he willed himself to focus on the matter at hand, questioning Peter Johns. He wondered how much of a New Hampshirite the guy was, considering his sister had motive to move to New York City. One of the quirky aspects of the state of New Hampshire is that its citizenry are an informed bunch, but adherence to a rugged individualism is of prime importance to the region, especially in the central portion of the state. Charlie laughed to himself and shook his head at the notion that many who aren't from the area think about the southern half of the state the way he used to, that it was nothing but a glorified northern suburb of Boston. Truth is, Charlie knew, that the people of the state were generally a warm and friendly demographic who valued personal freedom, responsibility, and a hearty work ethic. Charlie was loath to consider that he and his fellow New Hampshire residents were an isolationist, curmudgeonly bunch who just wanted to be left alone. Hopefully, Johns wasn't that type.

Charlie drove through Dover, then Richmond, then Farrington, and finally neared Laconia. Those places were in his rearview now, just like the brief reminiscence he had of his youth, driving through them. At the town's outskirts, he pulled off the road and dialed Peter Johns.

Johns answered.

"Hello," said a rough-sounding voice.

"Hi. Peter?"

"Who's this?"

The man's voice wasn't gentle. Charlie could hear it. Emily Willems couldn't hold a candle to this guy's delivery.

"I'm Charlie Redmond. I'm a police detective."

"What do you want?"

Defensive, no doubt about it, but not aristocratically so, like Emily Willems or Guy Davis. More like a weathered, chary tone, developed from harsh past experiences.

"I was hoping to speak to you about your sister, Wendy Cushman. Just for a few minutes."

"Got nothing to say. She's dead. Gone."

Boy, this dude was as coarse as sandpaper. "I need just a few minutes of your time, Peter. Promise. I'm in Laconia. Can I drop by?"

"Fine," Johns said. "But keep it quick."

Charlie drove to his street. He had to access it by taking a series of turns that led him to an alcove of similar prefabricated, skeletal-appearing edifices that could have followed in the next evolutionary step in the progression from mobile homes. Johns's house, in all of its slate gray, cubic, one-story splendor, was the first house Charlie encountered on his left. Charlie got out of his car as Peter Johns opened his front door. He was slight and disheveled, wearing a stained wifebeater and gray sweatpants. His unkempt attire and discourteous manner matched Charlie's initial impressions of the man. He looked many years Charlie's senior.

Johns didn't invite Charlie in, and instead directed him to sit on one of the front porch's dusty lawn chairs. Charlie declined.

"So you're investigating Wendy's murder," Peter said.

"Sure am. I'm thinking it's connected to another case I'm looking into. The murder of Lyle Willems."

"Don't know anything about my sister's death," he said, his face expressionless. "Only thing I know is she got bored of living up here and went to the big city and got hooked. That shit runs in our family."

"You mean drugs?" Charlie said.

"Yep."

Johns seemed to be speaking the truth. For all Charlie knew, drugs could have been a part of Johns's past, too.

"I suppose you don't know anything about the twenty-four-hour period surrounding her death," Charlie said. "Did you know her lover, a guy named Murray?"

"She never told me about no boyfriend. We hardly spoke, even when she lived closer to me here. She was a stranger to me."

Charlie couldn't understand the animosity in Peter Johns's voice. Sure, there was discord in all families. It's a universal sociological norm, he thought. But Johns spoke with such disdain, it was difficult to perceive the target of his emotion, his sister or himself.

"How about a guy named David Medice?" Charlie asked.

With that question, Johns's face softened slightly.

"Why the hell do you care about any of this?" Johns asked.

"I don't have a personal stake in your sister's death, Peter. I didn't even know her. But I do care about justice. I care about catching the person or persons who may be responsible for this so they'll pay for their horrible crimes. I care about you finding out the truth, because you may never get that chance otherwise."

Peter Johns was positively moved for the first time, his penetrating gaze leaving Charlie's face for a moment.

"Wait here a sec," Johns said.

I'm not going anywhere, remember? You won't even let me in your house.

He shut the door behind him and returned a few seconds later holding a picture of Wendy.

"I found this in Wendy's things, what little of them are left here. Cops said they didn't want or need it."

Charlie studied the picture. Inscribed on the back were the words *With the incredible David Medice.*

"It's Wendy's writing," Johns said.

Charlie turned the picture over. A smiling, radiant Wendy Cushman stood arm in arm with a younger-looking, thinner, fully coiffed David Medice. The photo was a little blurred, but Charlie was able to see both were surrounded by crew and cameras, probably on the set of *The Big Payday*. Medice sported a thick-lipped, goofy smile and 1960s-era horn-rimmed glasses, and appeared to be laughing hysterically.

Could be the perfect showbiz couple.

"Can I take this with me?" Charlie asked, hoping not in futility.

"No, you can't," said Johns. "It's all I have to remember her by. It's literally the only picture I have of her."

"I need it to get information out of someone. David Medice himself," Charlie said.

"No, I can't. I don't know you at all. What if I never see that picture again? I'm sorry, I just can't let go of it."

Charlie's smartphone's ringtone sounded out. He recognized Randi's number and excused himself.

"Charlie Redmond," he said.

"Hey, it's Randi."

"Hey."

"Okay, Wendy Cushman?"

"Right."

"She was an extra in *The Big Payday*."

"Thanks, Randi. You're awesome."

Charlie has a smartphone, so he could use his camera to take a photo of the photo.

CHAPTER 32

Charlie drove back to Portsmouth much faster than he'd driven to Laconia. He wasn't stopping at his bungalow, though. He was going straight to David Medice's place. The entire drive back home for Charlie was consumed by the certain fact that Medice was lying, and Charlie had to get him to prove it. Instead of taking State Highway 16 back to the heart of the city, he turned back north for a spell and drove up Gosling Road to Wedgewood and David Medice's address.

Charlie parked a quarter mile down the street from Medice's house. He thought about Wendy's pictures, the love letters, the television show *The Big Payday*.

Weird. Here's Medice, a guy who's smart enough to realize I could find out that he'd produced a show Wendy was in. But he never heard of her? Is he stupid? Does he think that I'm stupid? Could he have had a mental lapse of some sort that her credits would easily be accessible online? Could he be comfortable in his knowledge that he'd be safe from interrogation if extras' names weren't included in performance billing and credits?

This case is way fucking out there. Straight-up bizarre.

He slowly pulled up to Medice's driveway, still thinking.

This case is total bullshit. Just thinking about all the inconsistencies is giving me a headache. David Medice produced a TV show Wendy Cushman appeared in, took pics of her, and wrote love letters to her, but didn't know her? Lyle Willems had an affair, but he didn't? He went to a massage parlor, but he didn't? Total bullshit. Hell, Medice is too damn stupid to admit he knows her, even if he didn't kill her.

Charlie clutched the steering wheel so hard he got cramps.

Time to see how Medice handles what I've got in store for him.

Charlie walked toward Medice's front door and knocked. Medice opened the door.

"I thought you were gonna call me before coming," Medice said

"I lied," Charlie said, "just like you're doing." He walked past Medice into the house, nearly tripping over a low coffee table stacked with empty beer cans.

"What's going on? What are you talking about? Do you want to see the tickets?"

"Shut up. I know you knew Wendy Cushman."

"I never heard of her . . . until you told me about her," Medice said.

Charlie brought his face inches away from Medice's, so close he could smell Medice's morning pick-me-up. "Stop lying to me. I know you know her."

"Redmond, dude, I never heard of her."

"She was an extra in *The Big Payday*."

David Medice gave Charlie a hostile expression. "Just like every other loser chick who wanted to make it big in The Big Apple."

Charlie glared at Medice and said, "I saw the letters, the love letters with your name on them. She was in your TV show. She was incredibly beautiful. You knew her. You were in love with her." Charlie was practically nose to nose with Medice by this point.

Charlie was angry. But he could control his impatience with this guy. He had his reasons for dealing with him this way. He obliterated Medice's personal space. Practically close enough to kiss Medice, trying to get a confession out of him. Charlie wanted him to think he was about to explode. That this was all a bluff, sort of. Charlie was pissed, and damn tired of spinning his wheels with this case, no doubt about it. Charlie was the proverbial hamster running on the wheel, getting nowhere. He had to keep pushing this guy, showing him that he better not piss off this detective, because, well . . .

"What? I don't think so," Medice said. "I didn't even know her. And I sure as hell wasn't in love with her. Those letters weren't from me, dude. She may have had this crush on me, in her mind or something. But I wasn't in love with her. Never heard of her. And when she was killed, I was out of town. I'll show you the goddamn tickets and boarding pass receipts."

Charlie was going to get a confession from this weasel. He got even closer to Medice, like he was going to plant a tongue kiss right then and there. He dialed up the intensity in his eyes, spitting into Medice's.

"Bullshit," Charlie said. "Admit it, asshole. You knew her. Admit it now, or you'll wish you had."

Once he threatened Medice, Charlie knew he crossed a line. He tried to hold those personal feelings from becoming apparent. But now his thuggish performance was clashing with his true feelings. His true frustrations were being exposed. This made him feel vulnerable, as if everything he'd found out during this investigation was in jeopardy, that maybe he didn't know jack shit. Perhaps even if he did get something out of Medice, this whole scenario would come down to threatening some low-rent producer about a case Charlie wasn't even officially working on. Charlie took a deep breath. He couldn't turn back now.

Sensing Charlie's hesitation, Medice slowly removed his smartphone from his shirt's breast pocket, craning his neck backward to speak. "I don't know who the fuck you think you are or what you think you know. But if you don't get out of my face, out of my house, I'll call the *real* cops. I mean it."

"Great. Wonderful," Charlie said. "I'm sure they'd like all the information I have on you."

"Well, they can have it," said Medice, wincing with anger, "cause I haven't done a goddamn thing wrong. Unlike you . . . and your fuckin' police brutality."

Charlie took both of his hands and placed them on Medice's shoulders. "Tell me what you know, Medice."

Medice strained to wave the phone in his right hand. "Redmond, get the hell out of this house, or I'll call the cops. I mean it."

Charlie grabbed the phone out of Medice's hand. "I'm not buying it, Medice."

Did he buy his own bluff? Or was this still a bluff? Was he about to get violent with Medice's phone? The power surge running through his body gave Charlie uncertain energy.

He still held Medice's phone in his left hand. "The damn girl was in one of your stupid-ass TV shows. Any pea-brain could've discovered that, Medice."

"I never even set foot on the set of that reality show. It was shot, yes. I got a credit as producer, probably one of many, but I had nothing physically to do with that show. That's the business. Not to mention the performers who are extras."

Charlie held the phone, easily envisioning himself striking Medice with it. "Tell me what you know about Wendy Cushman, or this phone is going right upside your head."

Charlie was about to follow through with this threat.

"Wait," said Medice. He looked down at his pockets. Charlie moved back slightly. Medice reached into his right pants pocket and pulled out some tattered airline tickets.

Charlie gave them a cursory glance. They looked legit. They showed that Medice was in Boston at the time of Wendy Cushman's murder. Charlie was confused and still angry, but why? Was it the investigation at this point or the fact that Medice *did* have proof? Rather, this was evidence, he thought. Didn't prove that Medice didn't know Wendy. Hard evidence was good, but not in this case. Medice could use it to buttress his story. Charlie knew that he could find out what Medice's relationship with Wendy was, sooner or later, sure. But he would never have this chance, right at this second, right when he literally had Medice's back against the wall. Truth is, Charlie's trump card in the form of his bluff was waning in its power. The airline tickets had deflated any chance that Charlie could easily make this guy squeal. His chance at winning this battle was almost dead, like Wendy Cushman and Lyle Willems.

"You know," Charlie said, still in Medice's face, "those are easy to fake."

"Well, they aren't. Call the airline, or whatever. They're the real deal, asshole."

Charlie grabbed the tickets and threw them to the floor. He brushed up against Medice more firmly, eyes mere millimeters from Medice's face. He held up the phone, considering whether to strike Medice with it. The motivation to do even this was dying, just like his bluff.

Is Medice still feeling this?"

Who gives a shit you were out of town when she was killed? Admit that you knew her, you ass. Tell me about your relationship to Wendy Cushman."

Medice glared at Charlie. "You are in my house. You're threatening to hurt me, possibly kill me. Get. The. Fuck. Out."

Charlie took Medice by the throat, pushing his neck against the wall.

One last go at it.

But the rage was gone. The bluff? Still alive, enough for Charlie to know that this encounter wasn't exactly working the way he wanted. He pushed Medice's neck harder.

Charlie froze for a second. Looked at Medice, who was uncomfortable, but without expression. Charlie had no idea how to proceed. None. He stepped back from Medice and freed his neck. Medice remained standing directly against the wall. Charlie couldn't read Medice at all.

He took his eyes off Medice and looked at the tickets on the floor. He bent down, picked them up, and put them on the kitchen table, along with Medice's phone.

He walked back to where Medice was standing. He looked at Medice, who was standing a little ways from the wall against which he was pinned for dear life just minutes ago. Medice returned Charlie's glare, with a mix of relief, confusion, and some defiance.

Charlie decided to show himself out.

CHAPTER 33

Back at the bungalow, Charlie cycled through exhaustion, confusion, and anger.

Relax. Sit down. Think.

He went through a range of emotions not experienced in years, certainly not since the first love of his life, Jenna Walsh, was killed. Exhaustion, confusion, anger.

Summon your subconscious and think about this whole puzzle. It might be a big one, but there are a few enormous pieces that, once put into place, will allow you to solve the whole goddamn thing in a flash.

Charlie had to clear his harried mind, close his bloodshot eyes, and concentrate on the clues. He needed to think about the people, the circumstances, the implications about everything he'd uncovered this far. He had to unpack the tethers that were attached to each of these categories in his mind and begin to tie them together. What was the missing issue?

Charlie couldn't sit still. Exasperated, he changed his clothes and went out for a short run in the early evening. He was so focused he almost tripped over Thompson on the way out of the bungalow.

"Sorry, old boy," he said.

He immediately started running. Who, out of everyone he'd investigated, had the best reason to off Lyle Willems? His investigative sense told him that this wasn't some random killing. There had to be a way to connect the dots between all the people he'd interviewed and the places he'd seen during the investigation.

Two miles, and Charlie hardly noticed his rapid pace. He was focused on his mind, not his lungs, or his legs. He considered everything in this case, every last thing. Everything he knew, everyone he talked to, every place he'd been. He thought about those who personally knew Lyle Willems. He thought about all the tangents he'd encountered to build a case for the other murder that wasn't the primary focus of the murder he was hired to solve, Wendy Cushman, Bruce Baker, and David Medice.

David Medice . . . God almighty.

Charlie thought about the rant he used to attempt to scare Medice's confession out of him. Was he absolutely bonkers in even considering chasing down clues in a possibly unrelated cold case to begin with?

Four miles later, on his way back to the bungalow. Who really mattered in this case? Lyle's widow and her son only seemed interested in protecting their public images, as upstanding and morally righteous moneybags without skeletons in the closet. But what if the undermining stepson would try to alter the law to protect his mother's reputation? What else could he be capable of? Charlie kept thinking about Guy Davis's glass eye and shady mannerisms. Perhaps his paying off a detective was a ploy to get the cops out of the way. As in, he paid off a cop to protect his mother, but he says he didn't actually kill his stepfather ... or did he?

And what of Brenda Turner? So, she lied a couple of times. Okay. She was probably a harmless hospitality worker, infatuated by a charismatic millionaire. Lyle offered her a nice little payment to help her out and she'd accepted. Big deal.

Five miles, during the cool-down back toward the bungalow Charlie considered Larry Ash. What a joke this guy was. He'd hired a lame PI based on his paranoia that he'd land in hot water for doing business with Vincent Contadino.

And what the hell was Lyle Willems doing at a massage parlor . . . that damned massage parlor. The lesbian sex romp? Did he or didn't he even take part? Did some sex performer lie to Charlie about Willems even attending such a show? Did the Asian man connect to Lyle Willems's death, to Wendy Cushman, to David Medice . . . or to anything at all?

Charlie paced his front porch.

Carla. It would be so great to solve this case for Carla. Fundamentally, who killed Lyle Willems and why? She needs closure. I promised I'd give it to her. The one murder in Portsmouth that had any possible connection at all was Wendy Cushman's. But, that could be a crapshoot. So she and Lyle Willems got offed on the same day. So what?

He looked out at the Piscataqua. He had a fleeting thought of Carla. With all of this frustration and negativity swirling in his brain, he thought it'd be nice to actually solve the case for Carla. She deserved it. He looked toward the sky, imagining all the stars as representing different players in the case. He drew imaginary lines between them, trying to make new connections and constellations. Then it came to him: Medice. The Medice in the blurred picture with Wendy, the man with jet-black hair and old-school, horn-rimmed glasses, wasn't the same Medice as the TV producer Medice. Instead of the Big Dipper or Orion, Charlie would try to envision The Fucked Up Secret Underworld of Lyle Willems.

It was a flash of inspiration, but Charlie's mind was beyond frazzled, and he knew he'd get more answers once he'd gotten some sleep.

***

Charlie woke up early the following morning, and immediately his mind zeroed in on the case. Got to the kitchen and made coffee. He stood there, watching drops of brown liquid begin to fill the carafe. Mesmerizing drops. Focusing on the case. Drip, drip, drip. And that's when something in his mind, his subconscious, steered him into thinking of David Medice, out of the blue, the first realization.

Amazing what a good night's sleep can do for a detective.

He realized the man he'd tormented, the television producer David Medice, wasn't the David Medice in the picture with Wendy Cushman. That washed-up, unkempt, walking human hangover was innocent. He'd been truthful with Charlie. He'd never met Lyle Willems or Wendy Cushman.

Mental note: I'll have to apologize to him.

David Medice did share his name with the man in the picture, the man with a full head of jet-black hair, and horn-rimmed glasses, Wendy Cushman's lover. The David Medice that Charlie met and tortured was a diversion, a major one, who had absolutely nothing to do with the case. Yes, both Wendy Cushman and

David Medice *were* connected to a silly television show, but they never actually met each other. That's also when Charlie realized that the *other* David Medice, the one in the picture, was vital to solving the entire vexing puzzle.

Charlie's subconscious mind was connecting with his conscious one. He got a weird feeling in his mid-section with his thoughts. His instincts were now connecting with the logical connections he was beginning to make. He realized that the woman from the massage parlor, the performer, was honest with him, too. She'd never seen Lyle Willems before. She couldn't have. As a matter of fact, Charlie realized that Lyle Willems never even entered the massage parlor. Larry Ash was wrong. Ash had *thought* he'd seen Lyle Willems enter the building, his perception possibly clouded in a drug-induced haze. But Willems must've gone somewhere else. Charlie returned to the name David Medice. He rearranged the letters in his mind. He stared at the name in his head. Charlie looked at various objects in the kitchen: the coffeemaker, carafe, refrigerator, breadbox, microwave . . . but what he saw, mentally, was the name David Medice. The letters shifted around, taking different positions. They began to rearrange themselves into something new. Charlie relaxed his mind. Letting his subconscious talk to him, speak to him, in a new way. He thought about the words, the name, David Medice.

David. Dave. Medice. Med. Ice. Dave.

In his mind, he saw: DAVE MEDICE.

And then, he saw: DAVE MED ICE.

He rushed into the living area and grabbed a pen and a blank Post-it. Wrote down what he saw in his head. He shook his head and smiled at what he wrote.

He instantly knew the identity of the man in the picture with Wendy Cushman. The man who had written those love letters, the man who had gone to great lengths to disguise his appearance in that photo. The man who didn't go to the massage parlor, but to the adjacent dollar store for some items with which to disguise himself—a black wig, horn-rimmed glasses. That way, he could be in the presence of Wendy Cushman at a crowded party and take a completely new identity, in looks and in name. But he'd not chosen any old name. He chose the only name using words that described him perfectly. It was almost as if he wanted to leave a clue. He was too creative not to. That was his style.

Charlie looked at the very last grouping of letters he rearranged in his mind, in the name Dave Medice: A MED DEVICE.

CHAPTER 34

Charlie bolted for his Lincoln. He called Alfred Jenkins on his way to MedTec. It was a little past seven in the morning, but somehow, Charlie knew he'd answer.

"Hi, Al, you up?"

"Of course, my day starts at four. Like it does for a lot of productive geezers like me."

Charlie smiled. He really wasn't surprised. He asked Al to meet him as soon as possible, well, even sooner than that, like right this very second, preferably. "I'm there," Jenkins said.

Charlie parked his Lincoln directly in front of the MedTec building and waited. Didn't take long. Al Jenkins pulled up in his dual cab pickup minutes later.

As Al approached Charlie, he said, "You detectives keep all sorts of hours, don't you? Luckily, so do old farts like me who tinker with everything logistical around here."

"Al, I really appreciate your doing this for me. I'll let you know what I need as we go inside," Charlie said through his window.

"No problem. People here'll think that I'm in the office to work early today. Don't forget, there are lots of Type A's here. I'm one of them. But, I think you kinda figured that one out," Al said, smiling, as they walked in.

Inside Jenkins's office, Charlie told Al what he'd discovered: Lyle's secret affair with Wendy Cushman, the love letters, the disguise, Lyle Willems's double life.

"Al, this is one insane case," Charlie said, rubbing his eyes. "Nothing is as it seems. I really needed to talk to you again about this because you knew Lyle well. I mean, who knew what he was capable of? So, I guess what I want to know is, based upon everything I've told you, does it jibe with what you know about him?"

Jenkins thought for a second or two. "Well, we had a Christmas party once, but Lyle wanted to turn the idea of a run-of-the-mill holiday party on its head. Decided to make it a costume party instead. I've got some pictures stashed away I can show you."

Jenkins got up and took out a folder from his file cabinet, with photos from the party. He spread the photos out on the desk. In one of them, Jenkins was dressed as Casper the Ghost. Charlie noticed the man standing next to Jenkins resembled the man in the picture with that Wendy Cushman that her brother had showed him. Charlie's eyes widened.

"Lyle came to the party dressed as someone else," Jenkins said, pointing to the man next to him in the photo. "No one in particular, just some guy with thick black hair and horn-rimmed glasses. That was his costume. No one recognized him for a while. Everyone thought it was right up Lyle's vein of creativity. I sure as shit didn't expect it, but it was typical Lyle, being creative with people's minds."

"This help you out any?" Jenkins asked.

"You have no idea. Now I'm certain," Charlie said. "When Lyle Willems was with the girl I told you about,

Wendy, he went by a different name, a pseudonym—David Medice. This wasn't a random choice of names, mind you. Willems used the moniker 'A Med Device' to create the name Dave . . . David Medice—like in an anagram. Al, I think he was trying to hide his identity and presented himself to her as David Medice. Lyle would never be caught alive doing what he was doing with this woman, much less with any woman he wanted to keep closeted. He had a reputation to uphold, after all."

Jenkins nodded, momentarily speechless. Charlie pulled out the love letters.

"Here, read these."

Jenkins read and reread them . . . twice. "Whoa, Nelly, there's a lot in there. More than love. More like a lustful obsession."

"Right," Charlie said. "And Willems couldn't tell Wendy how he felt when he was Lyle Willems, wealthy medical device CEO, Portsmouth Central Country Club socialite, influential political megadonor and fundraiser. So he donned his costume, his alter ego, David Medice, when he was around her and had to tell her how he really felt about her."

"You think she knew his true identity?"

"Well," Charlie chuckled, "it's possible that his hairpiece may have slid a bit during their rough sex, if those letters are any indication. But I don't think it really mattered. While I don't know how or where they met, they each had a reason to have, to put it mildly, a sordid relationship. Wendy Cushman's partying, substance-fueled lifestyle was too exciting for Lyle to ignore. Whatever he was into, he probably needed a release, as those love letters suggested. She didn't really *know* him. Given her lifestyle at that point, I suspect she didn't even care."

Jenkins snorted a laugh at the suggestion and shook his head.

"But, honestly," Charlie said, "she was probably strung out most of the time. He could've benefited sexually because she was an addict. Hell, he probably paid for her blow and who knows what else. As long as he kept the affair hidden, and it looks like he went out of his way to do it, then he could continue to his heart's content."

Jenkins looked at the letters and the picture. Then he looked at Charlie.

"You read those letters pretty thoroughly," Charlie said. "It's obvious that those are honest feelings from a side to Lyle Willems that he was extremely careful to hide from everyone else. The ultimate costume, I suppose. In the end, the guy who wrote those letters was essentially a different person—David Medice, not Lyle Willems. It's just a crazy coincidence that his anagrammed name was actually the identity of another person, someone who had nothing to do with any of this. I think we've got an elaborate exercise in role-playing sexual deviancy and illegal drug debauchery. I wonder what Lyle would've done had he known the designation he came up with to hide his identity was actually a bona fide name."

"Holy Christ," Al said. "Those were a couple of kinky bastards. As for Lyle, I guess my worst fears about him are confirmed. He was creative, all right. Perhaps criminally so."

He wasn't the only kinky bastard I knew of.

Charlie smiled to himself. He knew he liked this guy. Charlie said good-bye and left Jenkins's office with the connections to the murder of Lyle Willems coming together.

CHAPTER 35

After he left MedTec, still in his Lincoln, Charlie called Steve Richards. He never needed Richards's help as much as he did now. Richards answered and listened as Charlie told him how the puzzle pieces were finally coming together. No bullshitting from Richards now. No silly jokes or double entendres from him, either. Richards was all ears, and, after hearing the update, Richards agreed to help him out.

Charlie hung up and drove to a Texaco not far from MedTec HQ: this was a call he'd have to pull over for. He pulled out the piece of paper Murray Stevens had given him at the conclusion of his initial visit with him, and dialed him up. Charlie was concentrating while the smartphone was ringing, gazing at the station's digital signage and wondering when fuel prices would ever recede. He heard the other end of the line pick up on speaker phone mode.

"This is Murray," he answered.

"It's Detective Charlie Redmond" Charlie said.

A few seconds passed without response from Murray. Then, a nanosecond before the silence would become awkward, Murray said, "Yes, the investigator. Hello. I wasn't expecting you to call. Or to get back to me so quickly."

Charlie said, "I was hoping to talk to you a little more." Charlie was trying to measure his words carefully. He didn't want to say too much.

"Okay, about what?"

"About David Medice."

"Medice. The guy you asked me about? I thought I already told you, I didn't know the guy."

Charlie had to use care, because he had to make sure Murray told him what he needed to hear. "Murray," Charlie said, "David Medice was having an affair with your former girlfriend, Wendy."

Murray waited a beat. "Okay, right," he said, an edge to his voice. "Are you calling to tell me I wasn't right about her not being involved with another man? Dude, I was just giving you my opinion. I mean, she was heavy into drugs. You know all that."

"Listen, Murray. Will you meet with me to discuss this a little more? I want to tell you a few things, but I think that I need to do it in person."

"Listen, I told you. I don't know a David Medice. If you're sure Wendy was having an affair with him, then maybe you should focus on him again. But if you've got questions for me, just ask me now . . . on the phone."

"This is about more than David Medice," Charlie said, careful about choosing the best words possible so they'd have the right effect on Murray Stevens. "All of this is about David Medice's affair with Wendy and how it led to her murder. I want to talk to you before I talk to the police. Before I talk to anyone else. Just you and me."

"I mean . . . Why?"

"Because you can tell me if I'm right."

"Right about what?"

"Right about who killed her."

Murray paused. "Where do you want to meet?"

"Wherever you want."

"I'll come to you," Murray said. "I don't want any more memories of my girlfriend's murder to be discussed in my house."

"You know where Rye Harbor is?" Charlie asked.

"The public beach? Off of Ocean Boulevard? Sure."

"Good," Charlie said. "We can meet there at the entrance. You can leave your memories at the beach."

Charlie clicked off the smartphone. He thought about all of the events in his investigation that led to where he found himself at this very moment, about the implications for all parties involved if his hunch turned out to be correct. He stared straight ahead at the service station in front of him, at the ordinary people just going about their day, getting gas, minding their own business. Just like he was minding his. He took a couple of deep breaths, in and out, slowly. He started the Lincoln and headed back to his bungalow.

***

Later that evening, as Charlie drove toward Rye Harbor State Park to meet Murray, he tried hard to focus. Doing so was more important now than ever. This is what it felt like to have all the pieces of the puzzle fall into place. To get the last puzzle piece to fit, he had to trust himself and his instincts. That was key. Trusting himself. He didn't want to think about the negatives, the what-ifs. He had to direct his energies to putting his plan into action. He drove toward the beach with the driver's side window down and let the early night-time air flood his senses. He felt good. He felt relaxed. Probably the most relaxed since he began the investigation that day Carla asked him to solve this damn puzzle.

He pulled the Lincoln into the beach's empty parking lot and got out. He was at an area that was lit, but dark enough to allow privacy from the parking lot as it gave way to trails leading to the ocean. His was the only vehicle in the otherwise empty lot. He got out and placed his hand into his right breast pocket to make sure he had the love letters from David Medice/Lyle Willems. Yes, they were there. He smiled.

He went to a nearby bench and sat and stared at the ocean. Minutes passed, but time seemed stagnant. Charlie's senses were so flooded by the sound of the waves that, had it not been for the headlights, he wouldn't have known that Murray Stevens was driving into the parking lot with his late model Range Rover to take Charlie up on his offer.

Murray got out of his vehicle. He parked about two spaces down from Charlie, but well within the illumination from a nearby parking lot light. As Murray approached Charlie, he looked huskier than Charlie remembered, the way you remember someone you've seen only once or twice before. His bulkiness was enhanced by the heavy jacket he wore to stave off the cool ocean air. Charlie wished he'd worn his jacket.

"Good evening, Murray," Charlie said.

"Detective, how are you?"

The two men stood facing each other for a moment or two. Then Charlie said, "I want to show you some things."

Murray stared at Charlie, following the detective's every move, without moving an inch himself. "Okay."

Murray and Charlie sat down on the same bench Charlie used earlier and Charlie took out the envelope that contained the love letters to Wendy that were from a man who disguised himself as David Medice. He placed the envelope on his lap. He didn't want to show the contents to Murray just yet.

"Before Wendy was killed, she was having an affair with the man we discussed, David Medice."

"You told me that already," Murray said, with that characteristic edginess he exhibited during the call with Charlie earlier in the day. "Did you bring me all this way to rub it in that my girlfriend was seeing some other man after we broke up?"

Charlie showed Murray the letters.

Murray looked at them one by one. He didn't read them in their entirety, just scanned them for what they were.

"Look, I told you she was with other guys." He glanced down at the letters. "I don't know who this dude David Medice is, and I really don't care. I mean, did you have me come here to prove to me that my dead ex-girlfriend was involved with some random dude?"

"No, I didn't have you come all the way here to tell you that. I wanted to tell you my theory on all of this."

"Redmond, I'm really not interested in your thoughts on Wendy's behaviors."

"Please, just listen," Charlie said. "It involves you."

Murray shifted his position on the bench.

Charlie took note. "Would you like to take a walk?" he asked.

Murray nodded, and the two men got up and walked toward the beach. The ambient environment was getting darker with each step. The moon was bright and it served as the only light they had as they advanced toward a small trail Charlie chose, feet from the shoreline.

Thank god it wasn't cloudy.

"The man who wrote those letters to Wendy went by the name of David Medice, but that wasn't his real name," Charlie said. "It was a name that was carefully thought out by the man himself. That man is dead now. His actual name was Lyle Willems."

"What the hell are you talking about, Redmond?"

They continued walking on the trail, approaching some large rocks. Waves pounded the shore, creating a louder noise threshold Charlie had to overcome with each step. They reached a mass of rocks.

Murray leaned against one of the rocks and looked at Charlie.

Charlie turned to Murray. "Lyle Willems, the medical device man whom you said you were familiar with, was living a double life. Everyone knew him as a successful CEO. That's how he presented himself most of the time. But he also led a clandestine life, dressed in disguise, as David Medice. He was in love with your ex-girlfriend. Lyle Willems, if you read what's in those letters, was desperately in love with her. Just like you were. Up till the day she was murdered."

"What's your point, Redmond?"

"There are many reasons, motives, for murder, Murray. Sometimes, people kill because they're bonkers. You know, like serial killers. Someone who kills someone else and stores all their body parts in a freezer, or something. That's fuckin' crazy. Other people kill out of fear, desperation. An example of this would be gang-related murders. Kids grow up poor and needy, and pissed off. Killing another is rational because it's the only way out of what they consider a shitty existence for them. They commit these murders under the guise of machismo, but what they're really feeling is fear. A fear of being killed themselves, or never amounting to anything worth a shit."

Murray stared at Charlie with a glazed-over appearance that projected either interest or languor in Charlie's diatribe. Charlie couldn't tell.

"Yet another reason for murder," Charlie continued, "is the one that's committed out of a crime of passion. I find this motive the most fascinating. Why? Because it's the work of someone you'd never think could commit a crime like this. It comes from the heart. It comes from a place of love. Sure, it's not a healthy, rational love. But it's love, nonetheless. When the person the killer loves is with someone else, it sparks an irrational emotion from the killer that can't be controlled. Sometimes, that reaction leads to murder."

The noise from the waves grew. The moonlight was bright. Bright enough for Charlie to perceive that Murray's expression morphed from a trancelike state to one of building anger.

A wave crashed into the beach. "Are you done?" Murray asked.

"No," Charlie said. "But what I'm about to tell you, you already know."

Charlie moved toward Murray, who rested against a large boulder. Murray stepped up off the rock to meet Charlie's advance. This is when Charlie had to trust his instincts. He had to trust that he was done right by his subconscious, that he placed all the pieces of the puzzle that fit, right up to this last piece, into all the right places.

"You killed Wendy Cushman, Murray. You also killed a man you thought was named David Medice."

"You're fucking insane," Murray growled.

Charlie wasn't intimidated. "You were still in love with Wendy. She enthralled you. She had that effect on everyone she met. You tried to hold on to her. But you couldn't. You couldn't let go of your love. One day, you caught Wendy and David together, and seeing her with him, another man, sickened you. Seeing her with someone who wasn't you. So you shot Wendy, twice, in the chest and in her face. You hit David—Lyle—over the head, knocked him out. Then you suffocated him. But you had time to think this one through, Murray. Very smart. You didn't want two people to be killed with bullets from the same weapon, so you killed the stranger by an alternate means.

"Then you found out who this man was, that it was Lyle Willems. Maybe from fishing around in his pants, getting his wallet, whatever. Once you did, you knew exactly how to dispose of the body, basically in front of everyone's face, out in the open. The fact that Lyle Willems was found dead at his own company was sure to confuse a helluva lot of people, including investigators. And so you took him to MedTec. You got rid of his disguise and knew to take his body to that location, because Lyle's company was a major source of funding for your startup, New England Science Today. I took the liberty of researching MedTec's library of grant proposals from small businesses. You actually stood to benefit greatly from Lyle's death, even if you didn't realize his true identity at the time you murdered him. Must've been a pleasant surprise for you when you did.

"During the grant proposal process, Lyle allowed you access to classified marketing projections for his soon-to-be-blockbuster spinal device for the grants you wrote. Besides Lyle Willems, you were the only other soul in the world who was privy to all of his secrets regarding the pending launch of the product. This knowledge would have given you and your company the ability to negotiate with his successor to reap every single financial windfall you'd have made sure was headed your way. Too good to be true, right Murray? But you needed to overcome some immediate obstacles first.

"You had to get him by security. But, you got lucky. MedTec security was lax that Friday night and early Saturday morning. They were probably screwing around, who knows? You probably found the keypad entry codes to disengage the alarm somewhere on Lyle Willems, then transported him in and left after you deposited his body. Of course, you took out a knife you had on you and plunged it into the left side of his neck to make it look like someone stabbed him right there, at his place of work. You were pretty lucky, indeed, that autopsy results were inconclusive and that the cops failed to pursue forensic leads, because little, if any, blood was found at the scene. No mention was made of a blow to the head that night. Very suspicious.

"And Wendy? Who the hell cared about her? She was a junkie, had no money, no job, no influence, and no family other than a brother who felt she was dead to him. She was just another urban street murder. No one would ever connect the two murders. And how could they? For all anyone knew, Wendy was having an affair with a man who effectively didn't exist."

Murray stared at Charlie. "That's the most ridiculous fucking thing I've ever heard."

"You killed two people, Murray. And you did it with the Zastava in your jacket pocket." He moved closer to Murray. "And I'm going to take that gun from you and compare the gun to the bullets found in your dead ex-girlfriend. They'll match, and you'll go to jail."

Charlie gingerly advanced toward Murray. As he got closer, he could see the combination of fear, anger, and resignation in Murray Stevens's face.

Murray pulled the Zastava from his right jacket pocket and pointed it at Charlie's head, its barrel situated about five feet from Charlie's face.

"Congratulations, Redmond," Murray said, his hands steady. "You figured it all out. Only thing is, what makes you think I won't kill you right here and now, like I killed them? Nobody's gonna know. Nobody's gonna hear the gun go off out here."

About twenty-five feet away, Steve Richards moved from behind one of the large rocks where he was hiding to another closer boulder. He listened as Charlie, moving closer to Murray Stevens, pulled a confession out of the killer. Richards kept his gun trained directly at Murray's chest the entire time. Charlie, at the barrel end of Murray's gun, a mere couple of feet from his face, heard Richards rustle. Murray didn't seem to hear anything, as all his concentration was directed toward Charlie. He also didn't notice the slight twitch of Charlie's right hand, motioning Richards to hang on just one more second.

Charlie knew Richards wanted to unload on Murray, but he obeyed Charlie's sign of caution and stayed behind the boulder, with his gun pointed at the killer, cocked and ready for action.

"C'mon, Murray," Charlie said. "Put down the gun." He took another step toward Murray.

"Take one more step and I swear I'll blow your god-damn head off, Redmond."

Charlie took another couple of slow, small steps toward Murray.

"You're not going to pull the trigger on me, Murray. You won't do it because your heart's not in it. Your heart isn't telling you to kill me. You won't. You can't."

Murray's face was dripping with sweat, his body shuddering. He clenched the gun harder and tighter. "I'm going to kill you, Redmond. You're a dead man. No one'll know. No one will hear this gun go off."

Charlie edged ever so closer to Murray.

Murray kept the gun aimed at Charlie. "I walked into Wendy's bedroom and a man I'd never seen before was on top of her, okay? They both looked wasted. They laughed as they looked at me. I drove home and got my gun and drove back to Wendy's, getting more pissed by the second. When I got back to her place, I shot her as soon as I got to her bedroom. Shot her in the damn face and chest. Soon as I killed her, I took the butt end of my gun and knocked out that motherfucker she was with. I pounded the side of his head only once. Turns out, that was all that was needed to kill the bastard. I didn't care, Redmond." He paused. "I didn't fucking care."

Charlie was no more than an inch or two from the barrel of Murray's gun.

Murray convulsed and perspired with a mixture of fear and anger. "I'm going to kill you, Redmond. I'm going to fucking kill you."

"No, no you're not," Charlie said.

Charlie swiped the gun away from Murray's right hand, and twisted Murray around, pushing him to the sand.

Richards sprang from behind the boulder, pinning Murray to the ground and handcuffing him. Just before he started reading Murray his Miranda rights, he turned to Charlie.

"You really *are* fucking insane, Redmond."

CHAPTER 36

A couple of weeks later, Charlie sat in Carla Willems's living room, wine goblet full of the local supermarket special in hand. He was fatigued, but satisfied. Satisfied with burying all the stress from the case. Carla sat at his feet, Tom purring on her lap. It was nice being with Carla and having the case solved. He felt good and relaxed.

"It seems like forever since I showed up at your place, introducing myself to you," Carla said.

"Yes, and here we are at your place. The ins and outs of an investigation can take a toll, that's for sure."

They both sipped their cheap wine. Tom slept and purred loudly, appearing as content as Charlie felt now.

"I had fun hiking with you that fateful day," Carla laughed, "in spite of the fact that my body was as stiff as a board for the next two or three days."

"You held your own on the trail. You could improve your skills with more endurance, though," Charlie said, smiling.

They ate a rotisserie chicken and fruit for brunch, other budget items Carla had bought at the supermarket for this occasion.

"Hey, I've got a crazy idea," Carla said. "Let's go out and take a walk. I think I can handle that."

They put down their glasses, and Tom scampered off into the kitchen.

Once outside, they reveled in the calmness about them, the bright blue sky and warm sunshine.

"It's been a while since I just stopped and smelled the roses," Carla said once they'd stepped outside.

"I know. Doesn't it feel good?"

The two walked for a few minutes, each looking around them, contemplating what to say to the other next. Any onlooker would have probably assumed that they were an item, out for a walk on a day as lovely as they appeared together. Charlie looked at Carla and gave her an encouraging smile. She seemed to gather that she could start the conversation, and he would gladly follow suit the best way he could.

"I'm so glad you took the case," she said. "I'm happy you figured things out and that I've finally found out the truth. I feel that coming to you, I've done something good, something moral, regardless of the horrible way my father conducted himself. In spite of all that, I still love him and wish he were still here. Maybe I'll never come to terms as to what drove him to do those heinous acts, but I honestly believe he loved my mother.

"Although my father apparently had this secret way about himself over and above simply cheating on my mother, I don't think that he ever wanted to hurt her. Maybe that's why he went to such great lengths to hide his affairs, and to hold on to his marriage to her. In his highly schematic mind he used the only method at which he truly excelled, his innate creativity, to try to protect himself . . . and my mother."

Instead it led to his pitiful and unnecessary demise.

Carla brushed away a few tears.

"You did do something good," Charlie agreed. She had helped him, in her own way, find the crucial pieces to solve the puzzle surrounding her father's murder. She was all the better for it. And her family, Charlie would admit, would benefit, too. Ultimately.

Emily Willems and Guy Davis finally had some closure, albeit not in the way they would have liked. Emily, Guy, and Carla were sure to benefit from the financial bonanza they were due at Lyle's passing. The stipulations in his will would see to that. But, they probably would have preferred that Lyle Willems's good name wasn't trotted out in the media and in the court of public opinion along with the secrets and dirty laundry that accompanied bringing the killer to justice. Although Emily was mostly right about how her husband had been murdered, the absolution brought by the case's closure did little to comfort her damaged self-esteem. All the money in the world wouldn't change that. In spite of the fallout, Carla indicated to Charlie that she would work to bridge the emotional divide between her and her mother; at least she was hopeful she could try.

Charlie thought back to the others related to the case. Bruce Baker, Wendy's super, finally had the news he'd been waiting for. Charlie knew that he was a stronger individual because of what had happened, and would continue to provide for his daughter as a single dad. The real David Medice threatened legal action against the Portsmouth PD, but had a change of heart once Charlie invited him to have brunch with him and Carla to formally apologize to him and discuss the investigation's conclusion. Once Medice was aware of the impact of

Lyle Willems's bizarre penchant for creating alter egos to hide his desire for maintaining extramarital affairs from those who loved and cared about him, he had a change of heart. Charlie was flattered when Medice even invited him to be an extra in one of his local television commercials. Charlie had yet to accept.

And Carla . . . When was the last time anyone heard about all the private pain Charlie went through at the time of his girlfriend Jenna's murder? Who had ever gotten him to face his true feelings about his divorce from his ex-wife, Rebecca? Charlie knew he still had a long way to go, and they had lots of ground to cover, but Charlie wanted her in his life, somehow. She made him feel hopeful, more than he'd ever felt before.

That, in a nutshell, was what was so precious about Carla. She allowed Charlie to overcome his poor emotional self-esteem. It was an issue that not only affected his ability to relate to the client who hired him, but also his willingness to solve one of the most challenging cases he'd ever taken on. Although he regretted the one-night stand with Darlene Connolly, he had reason to hope that both of them could remain friends. Darlene eventually contacted Charlie and assured him that their sexual encounter was water under the bridge. She said she really enjoyed talking expressionist art with mature men, and hoped she could get another chance at a discussion soon. Charlie made good on his promise to speak with her and apologize for the tryst.

"I honestly don't know that I would've solved this case had it been anyone else who hired me," Charlie said.

"Sometimes a missing piece of the puzzle isn't really missing, it's just being overlooked," Carla said. "The way you find it is to look at it, think about it, and talk it through."

Charlie nodded. He wanted to say more, but he felt comfortable just letting Carla have her say about all these things emotional and passionate. He was feeling hopeful about life, more than he'd ever felt before. For the first time in a long time, too long to fathom, Charlie felt that one day, he could get back into the relationship game and feel good about it.

They continued to walk and look at each other, returning to quiet contemplation.

It's all good.

This warm feeling he got with Carla today wasn't unlike the way he felt when he got on a running trail, a particularly challenging one, and knew he could use the land to his advantage, while preserving his strength and functioning. The elements wouldn't beat him. He would be in control.

He remembered Carla Willems arriving for the first time at his doorstep, looking at him with a quiet desperation. He remembered her shimmering skin on the beach that brilliant night, the lunch they'd had in Portsmouth Harbor, their discussion about writing creative nonfiction, and all those times they'd spoken on the phone. As he recalled those memories, he was immensely grateful that he could help her.

Or was it the other way around?

EPILOGUE

A month later, Charlie sat on his porch reading a draft of Carla's memoir, *The Woman I Am*. It was engaging, remarkable, sad, and inspiring. Like a memoir should be.

He'd planned to start the manuscript in the airport the next day, waiting to board his flight to New Zealand. But he couldn't wait. The manuscript Carla had copied for him begged his attention. He wanted to digest most of it before she took it to her editor for revision. He read through about a third of the draft before making the decision to go out for a ten-mile run, with hills. It was a great day for it. He felt stronger and happier than he'd been in months. He couldn't wait to expend even more energy on his postponed hiking sabbatical.

Charlie went inside his bungalow, gave Thompson a short petting, and placed Carla's manuscript in his carry-on for the plane tomorrow. He returned to the porch and saw Bainbridge working in her front yard, struggling with rocks in her wheelbarrow. She was singing some weird song that sounded like it was straight out of a speaker in an Indian restaurant. He shook his head and laughed.

Charlie walked over to the pull-up bar in the front yard and looked up. "You're all mine, motherfucker." Thirty consecutive pull-ups later, he jumped back to the ground and said, "Charlie Redmond's back, and he's better than ever."